THE SECRET CAVE

By

MARILOU WEAVER

MOODY PRESS
CHICAGO

© 1975 by
THE MOODY BIBLE INSTITUTE
OF CHICAGO

Library of Congress Cataloging in Publication Data
Weaver, Marilou.
 The secret cave.

 SUMMARY: Several episodes demonstrate how Micky
and Julie apply the principles of Christian living to their
everyday lives.
 [1. Christian life—Fiction. 2. Short stories]
I. Title.
PZ7.W3586Se [Fic] 75-26675
ISBN 0-8024-3829-6

Second Printing, 1977

THE SECRET CAVE

To

*Lori, Scotty, and Terry,
whose rapt attention when I first
told them these stories encouraged
me to put them on paper.*

CONTENTS

1

THE SECRET CAVE

Micky rushed into the kitchen where his mother was baking cookies one Saturday afternoon.

"Mom!" He sounded excited and out of breath. "Jerry's invited us to go swimming with them tomorrow. Can we go? Huh? Can we? You and Dad and Julie are invited too!"

"When do they want to go?" his mother asked him.

"Early in the morning. We'll take a picnic lunch and stay all day."

"Honey, tomorrow is Sunday," his mother told him. "We're going to Sunday school and church in the morning."

"Aw, Mom," Micky said, "we always go to Sunday school and church, and it's not any fun at all. I want to go swimming!"

"Well, I'm afraid we can't. It's more important to go to church."

"But why?" asked Micky. "It's more fun to go

9

swimming. Besides, sometimes it's boring in church."

"When we go to church," his mother answered, "we learn more about Jesus and His love for us and the way He helps us. We learn how we can love Him better—"

"Aw, Mom, OK." Micky went out to tell his friend.

Kicking a stone on his way home from Jerry's house that evening, Micky thought, *I sure wish I could go swimming.* "Oh, well," he said aloud, picking up a stick and running it along the fence, "maybe it will rain. Maybe they won't go after all."

But when he looked out the window the next morning, the sun was shining, and the birds were singing. It was a gorgeous day for swimming. Micky felt terrible. He did *not* want to go to church. He was angry at his folks for making him go. He wasn't very happy with Julie either. She wasn't happy either, because she wanted to go swimming too.

Feeling cross at the world, Micky sprinkled water from his glass on the cat who then ran yowling through the house, knocking against a chair that bumped the table and spilled the milk. This made his mother angry. His little brother was playing with Micky's new model airplane; and when Micky tried to take it away, Jonny fell over and

10

bumped his head and started to cry. Micky tried to explain to his mother, but his mother didn't listen; she just scolded him. He saw Julie smiling at him and thought she was glad his mother had scolded him. So he pulled her hair, and she slapped him.

Just then Micky's dad said, "Now listen here! I have had just about enough of this! You kids straighten up and act right and get ready for church. We're late already."

The whole family was upset. "Oh dear," Micky's mother said, "what a terrible way to start out for church. Everybody is so upset at everybody else that we won't learn a thing. Maybe we'd better stop right now and pray. Let's ask God to help us not feel so angry inside. Then we will worship Him the way we should." And she did just that.

Everyone felt a little better when she finished, and soon they were in the car on the way to church.

That morning, all the Sunday school classes met together so they could hear a special speaker, a missionary from the Philippines.

"I want to tell you about a special verse in the Bible that means a lot to me," he told the kids. "The apostle Paul tell us in Philippians 4:6, 'Don't worry about anything; instead, pray about everything.'*

*The Living Bible (Wheaton, Ill.: Tyndale, 1971).

"One day in the Philippines, I was driving along a very bumpy country trail in my jeep to a little village. I had copies of the Gospel of John that had just been published after being translated into the language of one group of tribal people. I was taking it for the people to read for themselves about God's love for them. They didn't know I was coming because there was no telephone or telegraph to tell them.

"Suddenly I seemed to be bumping along worse than usual, and I realized I had a flat tire. I stopped and changed it and continued on my way. But I hadn't gone far when I had a second flat. And then I was really in trouble. I had already used my spare. It was too far to walk to the village, and of course there were no service stations or tow trucks anywhere around. A scorching sun in a cloudless sky made me very thirsty, and I soon drank the little water I had left in my water jug. I looked around but could see no sign of people or houses.

"What could I do? Since the villagers ahead didn't know I was coming, they wouldn't miss me when I didn't arrive. How long would I be stranded there before someone came along? An hour passed, then two. I was beginning to get very worried. Then I thought of this verse, and I did just what Paul suggested. I prayed and told the Lord all about my problem. Of course He knew all about it already, but I think He wanted me to talk to Him about it anyway.

"Another hour went by. It wasn't so hot now. The sun was beginning to set. It would soon be dark. But somehow I didn't feel as worried. I knew that the Lord was taking care of me; and, if I had to spend the night there in that wild, deserted place, He would take care of me.

"Then in the stillness I heard a noise. Could it be? Yes, it was hoof beats. I turned around and saw a man on horseback coming up the trail. It was a cattle rancher I had met before. He greeted me, and I told him my trouble. He had no way to fix the tire, but he said I could ride on his horse with him to the village and stay there for the night. The next morning he would try to find someone who could help me. And he did.

"I have never forgotten that experience or that verse. Remember, it doesn't matter where you are or what trouble you are in, God is there with you. He doesn't want you to get worried or excited; He just wants you to tell Him about it. He will help you."

That's great for missionaries, Micky thought on the way home. *But after all, I would never get lost in any wilderness here in the States!*

Late that afternoon, Jerry came over to Micky's house. His nose was sunburned from swimming all day. "Mick, you really missed a great time at the lake," he said. "And you know who was there?"

Micky shook his head.

"Mac and his Pack."

"Mac and his Pack?" Micky looked puzzled.

"Yeah, you know, those guys that got kicked out of school last year for smoking pot. Mac's the leader so everyone calls them 'Mac and the Pack.' But they didn't stay long," he added. "Guess there wasn't enough action for them."

Micky grabbed his basketball. "Come on. Let's go shoot some baskets."

On their way out the door, Jerry caught up and said, "Mom said we could go again next Saturday so you and your folks could go with us. Think you can?" He lowered his voice to a whisper. "I found something to show you. It's a cave and no one knows about it but me!"

When Micky told Julie and they asked their mother, she said, "Why yes, I think we can all go to the lake next weekend."

Soon after breakfast the next Saturday, both families started out for the state park and the lake. After about an hour they arrived. Before the adults had even unpacked the things from the car, Micky was in his swimming trunks racing Jerry across one end of the lake. They even had a water fight with the girls. Suddenly it was time for lunch, and

14

everyone was glad because they had all worked up quite an appetite.

After lunch, the children decided to explore a little while their folks rested in the shade.

"Don't go too far," Jerry's father warned. "We want you to hear us call when it's time to go home. Besides, I've heard some thunder in the distance, and we might get a sudden shower."

"Hey, Micky!" Jerry called. "Come here." He called the girls too. "I have something to show you. Something special," he whispered and led the way through the trees. They followed him over a narrow trail that soon was almost hidden by underbrush which they had to push away with their hands.

"Here it is," Jerry said at last.

"Where?" asked Julie who couldn't see anything but some tall weeds and bushes.

Jerry laughed, and pushed away a small bush. Sure enough. There was the entrance to a cave.

"This can be a secret between us four," Jerry said. "I haven't told anyone else. Come on, let's explore it. I brought my flashlight." He stooped over and half walked, half crawled into the cave.

Just then the distant thunder suddenly turned into a summer storm, and the girls hastily followed Micky into the cave to get out of the rain. They were all huddled together listening to the rain when they heard another sound. A deep rumble which sounded like thunder grew louder and, before they knew what was happening, rocks and mud on the hillside above were loosened by the rain and came crashing down the hill, completely burying the entrance to the cave.

"Light! Turn on the light!" Pamela shrieked. Jerry groped for his flashlight. It wasn't very bright because it had been a long time since he had gotten new batteries.

At the same time, the children started yelling, "Help! Help!"

"It's no use," Jerry said at last. "No one can hear us. Worse yet, they won't even know where to look for us because they don't know where we are! What'll we do?"

"Maybe we can dig our way out," Micky said, starting to move some of the rocks with his hands. The girls joined him and began digging away the mud. But it was no use. There was just too much dirt and rock for them to move.

"Maybe there is another way out through the back of the cave," Julie suggested. So by the weak light of Jerry's flashlight, they checked the back of the cave. There was no opening at all, not even a small one. They were trapped!

Pamela felt her throat get tight. "They'll never find us," she sobbed, tears running down her cheeks. "We'll all just die here and no one will ever know. Oh," she cried, "I want to go home."

Then Micky remembered something. He could almost hear the missionary saying it. "No matter what happens," he had said, "remember God is always there with you. Tell Him all about the problem. He will help you."

"Listen, gang," he said. Because he sounded like he had just discovered something, they became very quiet and listened. "It's not going to do us any good to panic," he continued. "I want to tell you something. But first, let's sit down close together."

"OK." Even Julie had tears in her voice, and Pam was sniffing. She reached into her pocket for a tissue. "My scarf!" she exclaimed. "I can't find my new scarf. I know it was in my pocket." She started to sob. "It was my favorite and had my initial on it."

"Never mind, we'll look for it after we're found," Julie tried to reassure her, though she felt pretty scared herself.

"Remember the missionary in Sunday school last Sunday, Julie?" Micky was saying. "He said not to worry about anything but to pray about everything and God would help us, remember?" Micky went on to tell Pam and Jerry the story the missionary had told them.

When he finished, Jerry said, "Would God really

17

help us? We're just kids. Besides, Pam and I don't even go to church!"

"But that doesn't matter," Micky said. "God loves all of us. If He loved us so much to send Jesus to die for us, He loves us enough to help us get found! If you love Him as your Saviour, no matter where you are or what you're doing, you can talk to Him."

"Well, OK," Jerry said, but he didn't sound convinced. "But I don't know how He can help anyone find us when no one knows where we are."

"But *He* knows where we are," Micky said and began to pray.

"Dear Lord, no one knows where we are except You. We can't get out, and our parents will worry and we're scared. We don't know what to do. So please help us! You said in the Bible You would if we asked You and we sure do need it! Please help us not to be so scared. Amen."

"Maybe it would help if we sang some songs or told some stories," Julie suggested. Suddenly it was dark because the batteries in Jerry's flashlight had completely died. The four kids sat very close together, and Micky and Julie took turns telling the stories they remembered from Sunday school.

Meanwhile, their parents had packed up the picnic things and taken shelter in the cars during the brief storm. They called their children but there

18

was no answer. They looked and looked but couldn't find them.

Jerry's father, Mr. Schaff, was getting angry. "I told those kids not to go too far away. Now where can they be?"

"Maybe they found shelter some place during the storm," his wife said hopefully.

But no matter how loud they shouted, or how much they looked, they couldn't find a sign of the kids.

"I'll try to find the park police," Jerry's father said, now thoroughly worried.

"We have no idea where the kids are," Micky's mother admitted. "We can only pray that God will help us find them. Why don't we just ask Him right now?"

"You go ahead and pray while I call the police," said Mr. Schaff. He jumped in his car and its tires skidded as he drove out of the park.

Mrs. Schaff just looked embarrassed. "I don't know how to pray," she said at last. "We've never been to church to learn how." She was looking at the ground, and tears were running down her cheeks.

Mrs. Monroe put her arm around her shoulder. "You don't have to go to church to learn," she said. "God loves us very much and is right here with us.

19

You can just talk to Him like you are talking to me. I'll pray aloud for both of us.

"Lord," she said, "our children are lost and we're worried sick. You know where they are. Help them not to panic, and help us to find them. In Jesus' name, Amen."

While they were waiting for the police, they started searching again among the trees. "Did we follow this path before?" Micky's father asked as he started up a narrow trail. The women followed. They had to push away some of the brush to even find the trail, and it was very muddy.

Just then Pam's mother noticed something caught on a bush. "Look, this looks like— It is! It's Pam's new scarf! See, there's her initial!"

Then they heard Mr. Schaff calling. They hollered back, and soon he and two park service policemen carrying shovels caught up with them.

"Look, here's Pam's scarf," Mrs. Schaff told them. "They must be nearby. But the trail ends here."

"That looks like a fresh landslide," one of the policemen said. He and his partner started to dig with their shovels. "There's a cave behind this," he explained while digging. "They must have found shelter inside when the rain started and gotten caught in this landslide. I only hope we're in time," he added.

"A cave!" Pam's mother said. "Of course, now I remember. I heard Jerry and Pam talking about a cave the other day, but I didn't pay any attention and didn't remember it until now."

Just then the men broke through the mud and rocks. They shone their lights into the cave, and there leaning against the wall were the four children.

"Oh, they're dead!" moaned Pam's mother, starting to cry. The policemen crawled into the cave and quickly handed the children out. By then other rescue workers had arrived with oxygen. One man began to give oxygen to Jerry while two other men gave mouth-to-mouth resuscitation to the other three children.

"They're not dead," one of the men said, "but it sure was a close one. A few minutes more—" He didn't finish the sentence, but everyone knew what he meant.

Just then Julie opened her eyes. "Oh, Mom!" she cried. "You found us!"

"Jesus *did* hear and answer your prayer, Micky." Jerry was conscious and sitting up looking at his friend.

"You're sure lucky, lady," one of the park guards said. "From the way we found them, sitting together against the wall holding hands, they reacted

21

to this dangerous situation very sensibly. If they had panicked, they would have used up the available oxygen much sooner!"

On their way back to the car, Jerry turned to Micky. "Could I go to church with you tomorrow and learn more about Jesus? I want Him to be my Friend, too."

"Sure," Micky said, grinning.

The next morning his mother was just putting breakfast on the table when Micky came in all dressed for church.

"Michael!" his mother exclaimed. "You're all dressed and we haven't even eaten yet!"

"I know, Mom, but I can hardly wait to go over and pick up Jerry and the Schaffs."

"You sound different than you did last week! Sure you don't want to go swimming instead?"

"Aw, Mom. Sure it's more fun to go swimming, but we don't go to church for *fun*. We go to learn more about Jesus. I love Him so much, and He's been so good to me that I want Pam and Jerry to get to know Him too!"

2

PEN PALS ACROSS THE SEA

"I gotta run, Mom," Micky gulped, his mouth full of pie. "I promised Jerry I'd play basketball with him."

"Me too, Mom," Julie chimed in. "I'm going over to Pam's to study history."

"Now hold everything!" Micky's dad exclaimed, grabbing his son's arm before he could scoot out the door. "Before everyone tears off, I want a short family council."

"Aw, Dad." Micky sat down reluctantly. "Jerry'll be waiting."

"This won't take long." When he was sure he had their attention, Mr. Monroe opened a long white envelope and took out a letter and picture.

"Remember the missionary who spoke in church several weeks ago? I was talking to him afterward, and he told me about a family named the Wendells who are also in the Philippines. When I found out the Wendells have three children, a girl who is twelve, a boy who is nine—"

"Hey, just like us," Micky interrupted.

"Right!" his father said. That's what gave me an idea. Why don't we adopt them as our missionary family?"

"*Adopt* missionaries?" Mrs. Monroe sounded doubtful. "How do you do that?"

"We don't know any missionaries well," her husband continued. "By adopting the Wendells we could write to them and pray for them and really get to know them. In fact, just to learn more about them before we decide, I wrote to their mission headquarters asking for some information about them. They sent us their latest prayer letter and picture." Mr. Monroe passed the picture around and began to read the letter aloud.

Dear Friends,
　　We're here!
　　Where's here? In Sagunto, Philippines. But let me tell you how we got here in the first place.
　　As you know, we have come to live among the Agusan Manobo people. They have no written language so our first job will be to learn theirs well enough to write it down, analyze it, and eventually translate the Bible into it so they can read for themselves of God's love.

"Dad, isn't the Philippines near Hawaii?" Micky interrupted.

"It's closer to Vietnam and China," his father answered, "about 10,000 miles from here!" And he continued to read the letter.

To get here, we came by river barge that left early one morning. I had never ridden on a barge before and because I was excited, I was up before dawn and soon dressed. Then I woke Terry. Being only two, he is still bewildered and is always asking for Lori and Scotty who are away at school.

When we got to the dock it was just beginning to get light. I could see a big flat boat with a little cabin in the middle. When we got on board, I saw that on each side of the cabin there were two long narrow cupboards with sliding doors. These were the bunks where the crew slept. The captain graciously gave us one for Terry and me. Doug would sleep sitting up on deck.

Even before the sun came up, we started upriver. As we followed the twisting, turning stream, we saw clumps of bamboo houses that were little villages. Acres and acres of coconut plantations slipped by as well as dense, tangled, junglelike patches with no signs of people. Along the edge of the river, boys and their fathers fished from small canoes, or women washed clothes on the river bank, while the children and *carabao* (water buffalo) cooled off with a swim. All that day and for a while after it got dark we churned upriver. We pulled in along the bank to spend the night and started again before dawn the next day.

The middle of the next morning, Doug said, "Here we are."

"This can't be it. There's nothing here," I replied in dismay.

"The barge can't go any farther because the river is too shallow," Doug replied. "We'll have to get a truck from here."

Riding a lumber company logging truck is almost like riding a bucking bronco. I sat up front with the driver, but there were no doors so I had to hang onto Terry with one hand and onto the seat with the other. We were all very glad when we finally reached Sagunto!

The first thing I saw when we drove into the village was a clump of bamboo houses built on stilts. Our house, at least ten feet off the ground, seemed to be on the highest posts of all. We would be renting it from one of the villagers. All the people came running to greet us and help us unload.

Terry kept asking where Lori and Scotty were. It is hard for him to understand that they stayed at our headquarters to go to school. (I miss them too!)

That night as we lay down on our mattress on the floor (we didn't have a bed frame yet), we thanked the Lord for bringing us here safely. We thought of all the people who had visited us that afternoon who couldn't thank Him because they don't know Him. We prayed that the Lord would help us learn the language soon so we could tell them about Him.

When you pray for us, pray too for Lori and Scotty. This is their first time away from home.

In Christ,
Marie Wendell

When Mr. Monroe finished reading, everyone was quiet for a minute. Then Micky said, "Hey, if I wrote to Scotty, we could be pen pals and maybe he would send me some stamps for my collection!"

"That's a good idea," his father agreed. "Lori and Scotty's address is also on the letter so that shouldn't be hard."

Just then the doorbell rang. "That's probably Jerry," Micky exclaimed. "OK if I go now, Dad? I'll write later."

"Go ahead," his father said with a laugh.

Julie was looking at the Wendells' picture. "Wow! Lori sure has long hair. I wonder what she likes to do?"

"The only way to find out is to write and ask," her mother said.

Julie nodded, and was thoughtful as she went to get her books.

Enthusiastic about their new project, Julie wrote Lori and Micky managed to scribble off a hurried note to Scotty. Mrs. Monroe wrote to the Wendells, explaining their plan.

It seemed ages until they had an answer to their letters, but one night about a month later, Mrs. Monroe held up an envelope.

"Here it is! Want to hear what the Wendells have to say?"

Dear Monroes, all five of you!

How thrilling to be adopted! We like your idea and now that we've met you through your letter, we'd like to tell you a little more about our life here in Sagunto.

Do come into our house for a visit. Just leave your sandals outside the door by the others there. It is the custom here in many of the small villages to take off your shoes before entering someone's house. This is because it is often dusty or muddy outside and this way you don't track the dirt indoors.

Most people keep their floors waxed. They shine them by skating on them with a coconut husk. Besides, doesn't the floor feel lovely and cool to your bare feet? It is made of split bamboo. This is especially nice on hot days because even the smallest breeze can squeeze through the cracks and cool things off.

Please sit down. Would you like a Coke? It's

refreshing after a walk in the hot sun, though I'm sorry it isn't cold. We don't have a refrigerator or ice.

Don't step on that little lizard! They are friends. It seemed strange having them in the house at first, but they eat insects that fly in the doors and windows.

"Lizards? In the house?" Julie exclaimed. "Ugh! I don't think I'd like them or the bugs and insects."

Her mother smiled, nodding in agreement, then continued reading the letter.

What's the commotion outside? Oh, dear, two *carabaos* are fighting. Can you see them? There are two boys with sticks; they'll stop the fight. Everyone is watching the fight and no one sees that big old pig eating the rice they have put out to dry on mats in the sun.

"Hust! Hust! Get away from that rice!" He knows that means him! We just say "Shoo!" in English, but the Manobos have a special word for each animal that means "Shoo!" To the chickens they say, "Soo! Soo!" To the dogs, "Dya! Dya!" The *carabao* understand that "See!" with a click of the tongue means "Get moving!"

You got here just in time. We're in for a shower. Here it comes! And here come the goats, making a beeline for our house. It is built high off the ground and there is lumber piled under it, so it makes a grand shelter for them. But they also spend the night there! Ever try to sleep with goats bleating two feet under your bed?!

"Hey, a pet goat! That'd be neat," Micky said, grinning. "Just like living on a farm."

His mother continued to read:

> Come sit here on the porch and meet our neighbors. They often come to visit us and help us learn Manobo by pointing with their lip at something and then saying it for us to mimic. Sometimes we sound so funny they can't help laughing. And sometimes they shake their heads when we don't remember the words. It's hard to learn a language without books. But little by little we are getting there.
>
> Letters are a special treat, although mail is delivered by the riverboat captain only once a month. Tell us about your lives, what you're doing. You said in your letter that the leaves are beginning to change to crimson and gold. I can close my eyes and see them. Here the leaves are always green and we have only two seasons, the rainy and the dry.
>
> Thank you for your visit. We'll look forward to more—by letter!
>
> Lovingly,
> Marie

About a week later, both Micky and Julie had letters waiting for them after school. Micky's letter from Scotty was short and to the point.

Dear Micky,

Thanks for writing. You're the first pen pal I ever had. I collect stamps too. Here are some extra ones from the Philippines. It's Sunday afternoon and as soon as I write to Mom and Dad I can go swimming. We have to write them every week.

Write soon,
Your friend,
Scotty

Lori's letter to Julie was longer.

Dear Julie,

Thank you for your school picture. I have it on the bulletin board in the room I share with three other girls. There are two boarding homes for MK's (missionary kids) here at Nasuli. To make it more familylike, we have kids from all grades in each house. Scotty is in this house too.

I like it here pretty much. Our headquarters is in the country so we walk up the hill to school at 7:15 every morning and get out at noon. After a quick lunch we all race down to the deep, cold, swimming hole in the middle of the base to swim. It feels great! I've just learned to swim since we got here, but it's sink or swim since it is too deep to stand up in.

By 1:30 we're back in class until 3:10. We have about sixty kids in grades 1-8. I'm in the 7th, just like you, and Scotty is in grade 4.

Today I changed roommates. We do it every few months if we want to and it's nice having different girls to live with.

Please tell me more about your school.

Love ya!
Lori

"Mom, can you imagine, Lori has only sixty kids in eight grades! Wait till I tell her I go to a public middle school with 1,300 kids in grades 6-8! Wow! And think of swimming during lunch hour! If they are swimming in November, they must not have snow."

"I doubt if they ever have snow," Mrs. Monroe answered. "The Philippines is a tropical country, you know!"

Julie was thoughtful. "It must be really hard to have to leave your folks to go to school," she said after a minute. "I was homesick when I went to camp last summer, and that was only for two weeks!"

"I'm sure it is hard," her mother agreed. "And even though she doesn't say so, I'm sure Lori gets homesick too. You can help by writing her letters and by remembering to pray for her each day."

Julie nodded as she folded Lori's letter and put it back in the envelope.

3

PEANUT BUTTER AND
JELLY SANDWICHES

One day, Micky's mother got a letter from her mother, Micky's grandmother, saying she was sick in the hospital. She wanted Mrs. Monroe to come and stay with her for a few days.

"Oh dear," Mrs. Monroe said to Micky's father. "What will I do with the children?"

"Why don't you let them go to your aunt Melinda's while you're gone? It will only be for a few days and she loves kids."

"That's a good idea," Micky's mother agreed. So the next day after school, Micky and Julie went over to stay with their great-aunt Melinda.

"I know it is so hard for you poor children with your dear mother gone," their aunt told them. "So I'm going to let you do anything you want and eat anything you like."

"Good!" Micky exclaimed. "I like only peanut

butter and jelly sandwiches and hot dogs." And that's all he ate—even for breakfast!

Micky and Julie had a good time at their aunt's. A few days later when their mother returned, their father came to pick them up. It was almost suppertime when they got home. After they had sat down at the table and prayed, Micky took one look at the mashed potatoes, meat, salad, and vegetable and said, "I don't want any of this. I want a peanut butter and jelly sandwich!"

"We're not having peanut butter and jelly for supper," his mother said.

"I don't care. I don't like any of this. I want a hot dog!" Micky insisted.

"Goodness!" Micky's mother sounded surprised. "What's the matter! You used to like meat and potatoes."

"Well, I don't anymore. I like only peanut butter and jelly or hot dogs!"

"That's a shame," his mother said. "Because this is what we're having to eat and if you don't like it, you are out of luck."

This wasn't like his aunt at all, Micky thought. If he didn't like something at her house, she hurried to get him what he wanted. He'd show his mother. He just wouldn't eat. Then she would be sorry. So he said, "I'm not going to eat any of this food!"

"All right," his mother answered cheerfully. "You may be excused."

Micky got up from the table. He walked very slowly, expecting his mother to say, "Come on back, dear, and I'll get you your peanut butter and jelly." But his mother didn't call him at all. Instead she started serving his father and Julie.

Micky didn't know what to do because he was beginning to get hungry. "I don't care," he said to himself. "I'm not going to eat any of that old food."

He got pretty hungry that night.

The next morning, Saturday, he came down to breakfast and ate his cereal and milk which he liked anyway.

At lunchtime, he came in the house and saw that his mother had soup on the table.

"I want peanut butter and jelly," he said.

"Oh, I'm sorry, we're having soup," his mother told him. "Why don't you try it? It's really very good."

By then Micky, who had been playing hard all morning, was quite hungry. He tasted the soup. "Hmmmm. Not bad." He took another taste. It tasted so good that before he knew it, he had finished it all.

"Now that was pretty good, wasn't it?" his mother asked.

"Yes," Micky admitted. "But, Mom, why don't

you just serve peanut butter and jelly or hot dogs like we had at Aunt Melinda's?"

"Honey, I could serve you hot dogs and peanut butter all the time," she said. "But you know what? If that is all you ever ate, you would never learn how many delicious foods there are. You must always at least taste new foods. You might be surprised at how good they are."

Not long after this, Micky and his sister noticed a big moving van drive up to the house down the street and a man begin unloading furniture. Soon a car drove up and a family got out.

"Look, Mick!" Julie exclaimed. "They have a boy just about your age. And isn't that the cutest little girl? Let's go see them."

They hurried out the door and over to their neighbor's yard. There they discovered that Jorge and Malu and their family had just moved to the States from the Philippines. Micky and Julie knew a little about the Philippines from the Wendells. Their new friends could tell them even more.

One day Jorge said to Micky, "Can you come to my house for *merienda* this evening?"

"You mean supper?" Micky asked. "Sure. That'd be great. Let me ask Mom."

So Micky sat down to supper that night with his new friend. But instead of meat and potatoes, there were dishes and dishes of the strangest food he had ever seen. There was a big dish that looked like spaghetti but not exactly. There was another bowl with some kind of meat and vegetables mixed all together, and there were two platters of snowy rice.

At that moment, Micky wished he had a peanut butter and jelly sandwich. He was just about to say to Jorge, "I don't really want any of this stuff. Do you think I could just have a peanut butter sandwich with jelly?" Then he remembered what his mother had said about at least tasting the food before deciding you didn't like it.

Jorge's mother dished some food onto Micky's plate. Micky looked at it and thought, *This looks strange to me, but here goes. At least I'll taste it.* It was kind of spicy but didn't taste too bad after all. He took another bite. And then another.

"Would you like more?" Jorge's mother asked later.

"Yes, it's very good."

When he had finished, Jorge's mother passed him some ripe bananas and rice cakes.

Micky was getting ready to go home when Jorge came with him to the door and said, "Mama didn't want me to invite you over. She was afraid you wouldn't like our food. If you didn't, she would have been embarrassed because she hasn't learned how to cook American food. I had to beg and beg before she said yes. Jorge grinned at Micky. "I'm so glad you ate our food. Mama was so pleased!"

Micky smiled back. "Now it's your turn to come over and try our food."

"OK!" Jorge agreed.

On his way home, Micky wondered what would have happened if he had insisted on a peanut butter sandwich!

4

LITTLE BROTHERS ARE A NUISANCE!

One Saturday afternoon, Micky's best friend, Jerry, came over to play ball.

"There's milk and cookies for your snack," Micky's mother told the boys.

When they had finished eating and were on their way outside with the basketball, Micky's mother called to them, "Would you boys take Jonny outside and let him play with you?"

"Aw, Mom, do we have to?" Micky asked. "He's only four and he's too little to play our games. He just wrecks our fun!"

"He has no one else to play with," his mother answered. "If he's too little to play what you play, let him watch you."

"Can I play, Micky? Can I? Huh?" Jonny said, hopping excitedly first on one foot then the other.

"Oh, come on," Micky said in disgust, grabbing

the ball. "But if you aren't good, you'll have to leave!"

"I'll be good, Micky, honest."

"What a nuisance to have that pest tag along all the time," Micky whispered to Jerry as they went out the door. "I'll soon get rid of him, just watch me."

"But your mother said—" Jerry began.

"I know," Micky agreed, "but she doesn't have to put up with him!"

The boys played basketball for a little while and Jonny was content to watch. But after a few minutes he began to tease the boys to let him throw the ball too.

"Just once, Micky. Please?"

"OK, one time only," Micky told him. "But if I let you throw the ball, then you have to go play in your sandbox and leave us alone. Promise?"

"I promise," Jonny agreed. And he threw the ball at the hoop. It missed by a mile.

"Just once more, Micky. OK?"

"No, you had your turn."

"But I missed!"

"Yeah, and you'd miss again. And again. Now go play in the sandbox. You promised."

Digging his hands into his pockets and kicking at a stone as he went, Jonny left the two boys.

In the days that followed, Micky used every

trick and excuse he could think of to get out of playing with his little brother. Sometimes when he and Jerry played hide-and-seek with Jonny, they would hide so well that he could never find them. When he got tired of looking, they would sneak away and play without him.

One day when Jonny had looked all over, calling Micky and Jerry who never answered him, he finally gave up and went to sit down on the front steps of the house. There were no boys his age in the neighborhood and his brother wouldn't play with him, so he sat on the step and watched a long line of ants march across the sidewalk.

He was thinking so hard about the ants that he didn't hear three teenage boys call him. He jerked in surprise when one of them put a hand on his shoulder.

"Hey, kid," the tallest boy said, "whatcha doing?"

"Nothing."

"Why aren't you off playing with your friends?"

"Don't got any."

"Hey, that's too bad. Say, fellows," he said, turning to the two boys with him, "this kid doesn't have any friends. Shall we let him play with us?" He winked and poked the boy nearest him in the ribs with his elbow. The boy giggled.

"Yeah, Mac," he agreed.

41

The boy named Mac hunched down on the step beside Jonny. "Kid, we've got a really great new game we're gonna let you play with us."

Jonny looked up, his eyes sparkling.

The boy lowered his voice to a whisper, looking quickly around him as he did so. "But you must promise not to tell anyone. It's a *secret* game. Don't tell your mother or your father, OK?"

"And I won't tell Micky, either," promised Jonny.

"Here's what you do, kid—"

"My name's Jonny."

"OK, Jonny, you slip into the house. Make sure no one's looking. Then go upstairs to your mother's bedroom, find her purse, and bring us some money."

"But Mommy told me not to play with her purse," Jonny said, frowning.

"You aren't going to play with her purse, you're just going to 'borrow' a little money. Your mother won't mind. I'm sure she wants you to have it. Besides, we're going to take the money to the store and buy some ice cream, OK? Go ahead, we'll wait here," the boy coaxed.

Jonny still wasn't sure; but if Mac said so, it must be OK. After all, he was so much older than Jonny, almost a man, in fact.

So Jonny went in the house, found his mother's purse, and brought a dollar back with him.

The boys laughed with glee when they saw it and patted him on the back. "Atta boy, Jonny," they said. "You're a good kid!" Mac smiled slyly. "Let's get some ice cream, OK?"

"But I better tell my Mom so she'll know where I am," Jonny said.

"No! Don't do that," Mac said, sounding angry. Then, seeing that Jonny seemed about to cry, he added, "It's part of the game. Anyway, you're with us, and we'll take care of you and bring you back so she won't worry."

Reluctantly Jonny at last agreed.

A few minutes later, Micky and Jerry came into the kitchen where Micky's mother was baking cookies.

"Is Jonny with you?" she asked Micky.

"He was, but he wanted to play in the sandbox instead," Micky lied, taking a cookie. Satisfied, his mother went on with her baking.

A few days later, Johnny was again sitting on the front step. This time there were no ants, and he was wondering what he could do. Micky and Jerry had locked the door to Micky's room and wouldn't let him come in.

Then he saw Mac and his friends coming up the sidewalk. He didn't know whether to be sad or glad.

"Hi, kid," Mac called.

43

"I'm Jonny."

"Yeah, Jonny. Wanna have some fun, Jonny? Come with us. No, don't tell your mom," he added, as he saw Jonny about to enter the house.

So Jonny went with the boys to Mac's house. The boys had found a stray kitten that was dirty, bedraggled, and looked very hungry.

"We're gonna have some real fun, Jonny," Mac said with a wink. He caught the cat and held her tight while some of the boys tied some cans and stones to her tail. Then the boys laughed as she tried to run away but couldn't because of the weight on her tail.

Jonny didn't laugh. He felt sick. Without saying a word to the boys, and making sure they weren't looking, he slipped around the corner of the house and ran home as fast as he could.

That night he wasn't hungry even though his mother had fixed fried chicken, his favorite food. His mother felt his forehead, shook her head, said he must be catching the flu and hurried him off to bed.

About a week later, Jonny was just coming around the house when he saw Mac in the yard. He tried to run, but Mac caught his shirt.

"Hey, Jonny, where ya going? Aren't you going to say hi to your old friend Mac?"

"Hi, Mac," Jonny said, feeling very scared.

"You gonna play with us today, Jonny?" Mac asked, tightening his hold on Jonny's arm until it hurt.

Jonny swallowed hard.

"We've got some paper here, Jonny," Mac said, letting go of him and adding in a wheedling tone, "You don't go to school yet, do you, Jonny? But you're such a big boy, we're going to let you play with us, OK?"

Jonny began to feel better.

"We've got some paper here, Jonny," Mac said, pulling a notebook out of his pocket. "But we need a pen. Go get us a pen, Jonny. Get one of your dad's. Hurry. And don't tell anyone," he warned, squeezing Jonny's arm again. "Go on, kid, we just want to 'borrow' it."

Jonny's dad had told him never to play with his pen. But he had never said anything about not letting Mac borrow it, so it was probably OK. He sometimes let Micky borrow it.

So Jonny went into the house and got his dad's good pen and brought it outside.

"Thanks, Jonny," Mac said laughing as he put the pen in his pocket. "We'll see you later." He started to walk down the sidewalk.

"But that's my dad's pen!" Jonny cried, running after him. "Gimme my daddy's pen!"

"Later, kid," Mac laughed. "Later, when we're

finished with it." He poked his friends, and they started to laugh with him.

When the boys had gone, Jonny sat down on the step and began to cry.

His father found him there when he came home from work a few minutes later. Putting his briefcase down, he sat on the step beside Jonny and put his arm around him.

"Hey, what's the matter?" he asked kindly. "Did you hurt yourself?"

Jonny shook his head.

"Want to tell me about it?"

Jonny started to cry harder. But after a few minutes, interrupted by sobs, he told his dad the whole story.

Neither one of them noticed that Micky had come around the side of the house and was standing there listening.

When Jonny had finished and was crying quietly, his father looked up and saw Micky standing there.

"I guess it's my fault, Dad," Micky said, looking down at his shoes, his hands thrust in his pockets. "Mom asked me to play with him. But he's so little and can't play most of the stuff Jerry and I like, so I just pretended to play with him. I'm sure sorry."

"I know it's hard," his father said, reaching out his arm and pulling Micky close to him. "I know you can't play with Jonny all the time; but, perhaps if you made an effort to play with him part of the time, he would be content to play by himself and wouldn't go off with strange boys."

"Jonny," he said, turning to the little boy beside him, "Micky loves you. He wants to play with you. When he's playing things you can share or watch, you can play with him. Then later when he and Jerry want to play games that are hard for you, you play with your trucks in the sandbox, OK? If you see Mac and the boys again, you hurry in and tell Mommy."

Jonny nodded. His dad wiped the tears from his face and kissed his cheek.

"OK now?"

"OK." And Jonny smiled.

But they hadn't seen the last of Mac and his Pack.

5

RUNNING AWAY FROM HOME

It was one of those days. Nothing went right. Micky forgot his lunch money and had to borrow some from Jerry, who, for once, had extra. When it was time to hand in his math homework, he couldn't find it, although he *knew* he had put it in his book. The teacher made him stay after school and do it over.

When he got home and was eating cookies and milk, Jonny came up and made a grab for the cookie plate. Micky tried to get it from him but only succeeded in knocking over the carton of milk and spilling the cookies all over the floor. He tried to explain, but Jonny was screaming for a cookie and his mother just sent Micky to his room.

"She loves Jonny better than me," he muttered to himself. "He's little and cute and gets everything he wants. She has him, why does she need me? She doesn't!" he answered himself.

His throat felt tight and his eyes stung. "Well, I don't need her, or Jonny either!" He clenched his fists and walked over to the window.

"I'll show 'em. I'll run away from home!"

After supper that night while Julie watched TV and his mother put Jonny to bed, he slipped out the back door and started off down the driveway. He didn't really know where he was going, only that he was going away. Maybe he could get to his grandmother's house, although he wasn't exactly sure where it was. But it was a beautiful night and he walked quickly, looking back now and then to make sure no one saw him. He half hoped someone would notice he had left and call him back. But no one did.

And so he walked down the street, past the school, and on and on. At last he turned the corner, sure that his grandmother's house was on that street. But everything looked strange. Bright light and loud music were coming from a corner pizza shop, so Micky walked closer. Maybe he'd see someone he knew.

Just then the door opened and three fellows pushed their way out into the street. One of them was trying to sing a song very loud and off-key.

"Hey, Mac," one of them remarked, slapping the

49

singer on the shoulder. "You got talent, man! Real talent. How come you ain't on the tube? Then we could turn you off!" And he laughed loudly and coarsely.

Mac and his gang! thought Micky, feeling his stomach tighten into a knot. He slipped into a doorway and tried to make himself invisible. What if they came his way? He remembered Jonny.

The singer had stopped singing and turned angrily to his companion. With his open palm he slapped him across the mouth. "No respect. That's your trouble," he growled.

"Aw, Mac, I didn't mean nuthin'. You know I was only kidding," the boy whined.

"Well, watch it!"

With a sigh of relief Micky watched them turn around and walk in the other direction. But what if they came back? He'd go home. He turned around and started to run. On and on. But he couldn't remember which way he had come.

At last, out of breath, he stopped to look around. He was near the freight yards and he could hear the switch engines pulling and pushing the freight cars. Now and then there would be a clang, and then a whole series of clangs as another car was added to the train.

Now he was really scared. What could he do? Funny, but all at once part of a song from Sunday school popped into his head: "When you're scared just turn to Jesus." Well, it was worth a try.

Right where he was with his eyes wide open—he was too scared to close them—Micky prayed. It wasn't a bit fancy. "Jesus, help!" he prayed. "I did a dumb thing and ran away from home. Now I'm lost. And I'm so scared my legs feel like jelly and I can hardly breathe."

Just then he felt two arms grab him from behind and a gruff voice said, "Gotcha!" Micky turned his head and what he saw almost made his heart stop beating. He had read about hoboes who rode the freights, but he had never seen one before. This one had scraggly whiskers, old clothes, and didn't smell very good.

"Let me go!" Micky screamed, finding his voice at last.

"Shut up!" the man said, clamping his hand over Micky's mouth. "Wanna bring the cops down on us?" And he picked up the struggling boy and carried him through some bushes up a narrow path.

After what seemed like a long time, Micky saw a light which turned out to be a small fire. The man put him down and laughed.

"Hey, Fargo, look what I found!" There were two other men sitting around the fire. The man named Fargo looked up and frowned.

"He was standing like a scared rabbit down near

the freights. He looked like he was about to start hollering for help, and you know what that would do. We don't need the law around here."

Fargo didn't say anything for a while. He just looked at Micky. But he didn't seem as mean as the other men, and somehow, watching him, Micky felt a tiny bit better.

"What're you doing in this part of town at this time of night, kid?" Fargo asked at last.

"Running away from home," Micky answered in a small voice. All at once he wished more than anything in his life that he were home in bed. But of course he wasn't. What would these men do to him? Had his folks missed him yet? But even if they had, they wouldn't know where to look for him. Micky felt sick. Deep down inside, he felt sick.

"Sit down," Fargo ordered. The other two were making jokes about him, but Fargo said, "Quiet! I want to hear the kid's story."

"My name is Micky," he said when he had sat down crosslegged on the ground. "I have a big sister, Julie, and a little brother, Jonny."

"So why did you run away?" Fargo asked gently.

"Mom loves Jonny and Julie better'n me. That's why."

"How do you know?"

"Well, Julie gets to stay up later than I do and

52

watch more TV. She often goes to parties at church and school and stays overnight with her friends. And Jonny does lots of things like spilling his milk and breaking my toys, and Mom doesn't even scold him." He told Fargo about the carton of milk and everything else that had happened that day. He talked for a long time. When he finally stopped and looked up, Fargo was gazing into the fire that was now only a few coals. Micky could hardly see his face in the dark.

At last he looked up and said, "Kid, I'm sure it doesn't seem like it today, but your mom loves you, she really does. You're lucky. I didn't have a mom and dad. They were both killed when I was smaller than Jonny. I went to live with an aunt who already had seven kids of her own. Another one she didn't need, and she said so. When I got older she threw me out of the house and I haven't been back since."

He paused and then said gruffly, "Come on, kid, I'll take you home. Your folks are probably worried sick."

He stood up, said something to his companions, then took Micky by the hand.

It seemed like they walked for a long time. Fargo didn't say anything else, and although Micky wanted to ask him a lot of questions about riding the rails and being a hobo, he didn't.

At last they came to Micky's school. "Can you find your way from here, kid?" Fargo asked. "Your folks would call the cops for sure if they saw me standing at the door with you. Go on now. Don't be scared. I'll watch you from here."

Micky started running toward home. When he got close to the house, he slowed down, out of breath, and turned around. He could see Fargo standing by a tree. He waved to him, then turned and hurried up the steps.

Fargo was right. His folks *were* worried, and they were glad to see him home safely. But Micky thought they weren't half as glad to have him home as he was to be there.

6

LOG RUSTLERS

"Michael! Come back and sit down," Micky's father called as Micky tried to slip upstairs unnoticed. "We're not finished with supper. We have to go over our verses and pray. Then you can be excused."

"Aw, Dad. Jerry said the fellows would be at his house by 6:30, and it's already 6:15. I'll be late."

"This won't take long."

Reluctantly Micky came back and sat down at the table. Each night after supper the Monroes repeated a Bible verse together, learning several new ones each week. Tonight the verse was Psalm 3:5: "Then I lay down and slept in peace and woke up safely, for the Lord was watching over me."*

His elbows on the table, his head in his hands, Micky barely mumbled the words, hardly hearing them, he was so impatient to be gone.

*The Living Bible.

"Micky," his father said gently, "I know you think this is a waste of time. I know you'd rather be outside with the guys. But why do you think we bother to learn these verses anyway?"

"I dunno," Micky muttered, staring at the table.

"We store verses in our brains, which are like computers. When we need help, guidance, or encouragement, the Lord can bring them back into our thoughts. But He can't do this if we haven't put them there in the first place."

"Hey, like I remembered the Sunday school song the night I ran away and was so scared," Micky exclaimed. Then he added, "I forgot to tell you. I saw Mac and his gang that night by a pizza shop. I was afraid they would come my way, and they weren't in a very good mood. Dad," he said thoughtfully after a pause, "let's pray for Mac. He sure needs help."

"Pray for Mac?" Julie asked. "He's beyond help," she added scornfully.

"No one is ever beyond help in God's eyes, honey," her mother said gently. "And never underestimate the power of your prayers."

They repeated their verse again, then Mr. Monroe asked for other prayer requests. Julie had a history test the next day she was dreading. Mrs. Monroe mentioned a sick neighbor she would later be taking supper to. And of course they prayed for their missionary friends, the Wendells.

Although it took only a few minutes, it seemed like ages to Micky who knew he'd be late to Jerry's. As it turned out, he was the first of the guys to arrive for the basketball game in Jerry's backyard.

After supper about a week later, Mr. Monroe pulled a letter out of his pocket. "We got quite an exciting letter from the Wendells today," he said and then began to read.

Dear Monroes, all five of you!

Did you know that we have rustlers? Not cattle rustlers, but log rustlers. The loggers here cut logs far up in the mountains. If they have fifty to a hundred logs, they cable them together into huge rafts which are towed by launch to the city. If there are only a few logs, they float down river by themselves. Before they are dragged by *carabao* down to the river, however, each log is branded so that the owner can easily pick his out from the other logs. Our neighbor's brand, for instance, is LL for Lalong Litera, his name.

Log rustlers will often wait along the river in canoes where the underbrush is dense and there are no houses. As the logs float by, the thieves pick out the ones they want, rope them, and pull them up one of the many small streams that flow into the river. Along these streams there are quiet little ponds almost surrounded by trees and dense shrubs. Here the log rustlers change the brands on the logs, then cover them with leaves and brush. Several weeks later, when the search has died down, they cut up the logs and float them down river to the sea.

There is a big lumber company near us that cuts and ships a great number of logs to the coast. Because thieves have made river raids and stolen their logs, they station men called "concession guards" up and down the river to protect their interests.

Last night, our neighbor came over with startling news. Two days ago, pirates had boarded a launch towing a huge log raft to the port city. They had planned to rob a wealthy Chinese merchant on board, but he had transferred to a canoe with an outboard motor a short time before.

The thieves, frustrated in their attempt, killed three of the crew and made off with the log raft. Everyone has been on edge since the killers are supposed to be in this area. Then last night, our neighbor told us, one of the log rustlers was shot in a nearby village by the police constabulary. The rest are still on the loose. He warned us to lock our door and not let anyone in.

The rustlers had no reason to bother us. On the other hand, the idea is prevalent that all Americans are rich, and indeed we do have more than most of the town folks. Frustrated in their attempt to rob the merchant, would they try us instead? We had no way of knowing.

Since we have no electricity and only a kerosene lantern, we don't usually stay up very late at night. Even before the sun is up in the morning, the roosters crow, the dogs bark, and the people begin to wake up and get ready for a new day.

But it was very dark with the lantern off. There was no moon. And as I lay in bed, I could hear all kinds of strange sounds. I thought of stories I had heard of raiders who had attacked villagers at night and speared the sleeping occupants through cracks in the split bamboo floor. I was glad we had a wooden bed several feet off the floor. The neighbor's dog barked, and I wondered if he were barking at intruders.

I have never felt quite so alone, even though Doug was there with me. There was no place we could go and no one we could call for help.

"Doug, I can't sleep," I said at last. He was awake too.

"What's wrong?" he asked, as if he didn't know!

"I hear so many strange sounds I never noticed before."

"You're scared!"

"Yes," I had to admit.

He took my hand and reminded me of the verse we had read in devotions that morning. "Then I lay down and slept in peace and woke up safely for the Lord was watching over me."* Then Doug

*The Living Bible.

59

prayed, committing us to the Lord's care. And a funny thing happened. The fear drained out of me and I felt a strange kind of peace that was like a gift from the Lord.

Know something? We both went right to sleep and didn't wake until 4:30 when our neighbor turned on his transistor radio (the only one in the village) full blast! The Lord had kept His promise!

But I think it was your prayers that helped too. What if we hadn't just read that verse? What if we hadn't asked the Lord's help? I'm sure I would have stayed awake all night listening to the sounds around us. . . .

"Hey, that's the same verse we learned last week," Micky interrupted in surprise. He looked thoughtful, remembering what his father had said.

Later, after they had prayed, his father stood up, came around the table and gave Micky's shoulder a quick squeeze. Mr. Monroe didn't say anything. He didn't have to. They both knew what Micky was thinking.

But neither of them knew then of another prayer God would use Micky to answer.

7

DOING THINGS YOUR
OWN WAY

"Kids," Micky's mother said one Saturday morning as she got ready to walk out the front door. "I have some shopping to do and I may be a little late. If I'm not back in time, fix yourselves some sandwiches for lunch. And don't let any strangers in the house," she added, remembering Jonny's encounter with Mac and his boys.

"OK," Julie called.

"Say, Julie," Micky said when the door had closed and their mother had gone. "Don't you sometimes wonder why parents always bug their kids about manners? If it's not, 'Get your elbows off the table,' or 'Don't talk with your mouth full,' it's 'Don't take such big bites!'"

"Yeah," Julie agreed. "You can't even eat in peace without somebody saying, 'Don't use your fingers!' or 'Use your napkin!'"

"If Mom isn't here for lunch, let's throw out our manners and enjoy ourselves. OK?"

"Sure," Julie agreed. "I think manners are a drag anyway."

The morning passed swiftly and soon it was time for lunch. Micky and Julie were hungry and since their mother wasn't home yet, they fixed their own lunch and sat down to eat without her.

Micky started to reach for some food when Julie said, "Well, we really should pray first, don'tcha think? I mean, thanking God for the food isn't exactly manners, is it?"

So Julie thanked the Lord for the food. Just then the doorbell rang. "Come in, it's open!" Micky yelled.

"I'm looking for your mother," Aunt Sara said, walking into the kitchen. "Is she here?"

"Nope," Micky said, spreading a piece of bread with peanut butter.

"She's shopping and said she might be late for lunch," Julie added.

"I do need to see her," Aunt Sara said as if to herself. "I need the pattern she promised me so I can make my dress this afternoon. Maybe I'll just stay and wait for her." And she sat down on one of the kitchen stools.

"Wanna sandwich?" Julie asked, her mouth full.

"Why, yes. That would be nice."

"There's a plate in the cupboard," Micky mumbled. Both of his elbows were on the table and he was stuffing his mouth with both hands.

Aunt Sara got a plate and started to make herself a sandwich while Micky and Julie, true to their resolve not to remember their manners, raced to see who could eat the most in the shortest amount of time.

Aunt Sara watched them in silence for a few minutes. No one offered her anything so she had to help herself.

"I guess I won't stay after all," she said after only a couple of bites of her sandwich.

"Suit yourself," Julie said, not looking up from her plate.

Just then the door opened and their mother walked in, her arms full of groceries.

"Hi, Sue," Aunt Sara said when she saw her, "I came to borrow that pattern you promised me."

"I'll get it right away." Mrs. Monroe put the groceries on the table, and she and Aunt Sara went off together.

Micky and Julie got up from the table and went out to play.

"That was great," Micky said, grinning. "No worrying about manners every minute."

Julie agreed. "Funny Aunt Sara didn't seem very

hungry." But the children soon forgot all about the incident.

Several days later their mother said to them, "Dad and I are going out to dinner tonight. You kids can watch TV until 8:30, then get to bed. Sally will be here to stay with you and put Jonny to bed."

"Where are you going, Mom?" Julie asked.

"We're going to Aunt Sara's for barbecue," her mother answered.

"Barbecue at Aunt Sara's?" Micky exclaimed. "That's keen. Why can't we go?"

"Kids, I just don't know. It's very strange but the last thing Aunt Sara said to me was, 'I think we won't include the children this time.' I don't know what could have made her say that."

Julie and Micky looked at each other.

"She has always included you children when she has invited us before," their mother went on, shaking her head.

After their parents had gone, Micky came to Julie and said, "I've been thinking. You don't suppose something we said or did at the table that day Aunt Sara was here made her not invite us, do ya?"

"That was the day we were doing without our manners. Maybe that's what turned her off."

"I'm afraid so," Micky agreed. "Maybe it wasn't such a good idea after all. Man, I wish we could have gone tonight. It's always such fun at Aunt Sara's house."

Restless, Micky snapped on the TV to hear a newscaster saying, "Police are investigating rumors that the abandoned McKeever house near Sunnyside Park is the hangout for drug pushers and junkies. The McKeever house will be torn down next spring to make way for the new interstate highway. In the Far East. . . ."

"Turn it off," Julie called from the kitchen. "No news is ever good, so why listen to so much bad?"

Micky turned off the set and came into the kitchen where Julie was filling the dishwasher.

"I'll bet Mac's a pusher," Micky said thoughtfully. "Where else does he get money? He always seems to have plenty and I'm sure he doesn't work for it."

"Not that you could tell it by the same pair of **blue** jeans he wears year in and year out!" Julie said with a laugh. "So far our prayers for him haven't done much good," she added.

"Yeah," Micky agreed, "but maybe God isn't as impatient as we are."

The evening dragged by even though their parents came home early.

The next morning at breakfast, Julie asked her mother about the barbecue at Aunt Sara's.

"We had a good time," her mother answered. "But we missed you. I wish you could have come."

"Mom," Julie said, "I think we know why Aunt Sara didn't invite us this time. The day she came to visit and stayed for lunch, Micky and I decided before she came we would forget about our manners. I mean, they seem like such a bother and we thought we would enjoy our food and not worry about them for once."

"I guess we weren't very polite," Micky agreed. "We talked with our mouths full, and we kept our elbows on the table. You know, we did all the things you always tell us not to. Maybe that's why Aunt Sara made you leave us home."

"Oh, dear, I'm afraid you're right," their mother said.

"But, Mom, what can we do about it now? I mean we aren't really like that. It was just for that one day we forgot our manners. But we really do know how we're supposed to act."

"I'll tell you what," their mother suggested. "Let's invite Aunt Sara and Uncle Joe over here for dinner one evening. You get your manners out and dust them off and show them you know how to behave. Maybe if Aunt Sara sees she was mistaken, she'll invite you next time."

"That's a good idea," the childen agreed.

So a few days later, **Julie and Micky**, all dressed in their best clothes, were anxiously waiting for their aunt and uncle. The doorbell rang and Micky went to answer it.

"Good evening, Uncle Joe and Aunt Sara," he said. "Won't you please come in?"

Aunt Sara looked surprised but didn't say anything.

That night at supper, Julie and Micky did their best. They not only remembered their table manners, but they said "please" and "thank you" without any prompting from their mother. They were so polite they seemed like different children, and they noticed Aunt Sara watching them throughout the meal.

Later as Uncle Joe and Aunt Sara were getting ready to go home, the children heard Aunt Sara talking to their mother. "Sue," she said, "I just don't understand it. Your children are so well behaved. When I was here for lunch I thought they were the most unruly, spoiled children I had seen in a long time. I didn't want them in my house! But tonight their manners were perfect, and you didn't have to say anything to them!"

"Yes, I know," their mother smiled. "The day you were here was a sort of experiment that didn't work out. Why don't we just forget all about it?"

"One of these days we'll be having another barbecue," Aunt Sara was saying. "And this time, please do bring Micky and Julie."

Micky turned to Julie and winked. Julie just smiled.

8

EVEN WHEN YOU DON'T WANT TO!

Micky and Jerry were on their way home from school.

"Mac's done it again." Jerry tossed the baseball he was carrying up in the air and caught it with one hand.

"Done what?" Micky wanted to know.

"Stolen a car!"

"Did they arrest him?"

"Nope. Actually he didn't steal it, I guess he just borrowed it for a few hours. It was the school principal's car, that's how come the guys were talking about it."

He paused to toss Micky the ball, then continued. "Actually Mr. Saunders would never have known except that when he went to get in his car this morning, he noticed that the front fender had a big dent."

"How does he know Mac did it?" Micky asked, stopping in the middle of the walk, the ball in his hand.

"He can't prove Mac did it, but he saw him and the Pack hanging around the corner drugstore when he came home after the PTA meeting."

"We've been praying for Mac every night but instead of getting better, he gets worse!"

"Maybe God just hasn't gotten through to him yet."

Jerry caught the ball Micky threw him and continued down the walk. "Can you play baseball with us today?" he asked. "I'll let you use my new mitt. I hope I can be catcher on the team this year! Leave your things at home and stop by my house. We'll go together."

"OK," Micky agreed and started to walk faster.

"By the way," Jerry said, catching up to him. "Remember that new guy, Mark what's-his-name who broke his leg the second day he was in school? One of the guys said he came home from the hospital yesterday but the doctor won't let him come to school until Monday."

Just then they reached Micky's house.

"See ya soon," he called to Jerry as he rushed up the steps.

His mother was in the kitchen and had already

poured him a glass of milk. There was a plate of cookies on the table too, his favorite kind.

"I hope you've finished your homework," she said. "I have something I want you to do for me this afternoon.

"Hope it won't take long," Micky said, his mouth full of cookies. "I'm going to play baseball with Jerry and the guys."

"Do you remember Mark, the new boy who broke his ankle?" his mother asked.

Micky nodded and reached for another cookie.

"His mother called and wondered if you could come over and play some games or something with him this afternoon."

"Aw, Mom, why me?"

"We're practically neighbors, you know. I mean, they just live down the block."

"Aw, Mom, I hardly know him. Besides, I promised Jerry I'd play ball with him and he's going to let me use his new mitt."

"Mark's dad had to move in the middle of the school year so Mark had to leave all his friends behind. And before he had a chance to make new ones, he fell and broke his leg. He's very lonely, especially since he can't get out and play. He remembers you because you walked him to school a couple of times and he wants you to come over and visit."

71

Micky did *not* want to go. He had been looking forward to playing ball. Sitting inside on a sunny day and playing games with a boy he hardly knew did not sound like his idea of a good time. But somehow he knew deep inside that it was the right thing to do and at last he said, "Oh, all right. I'll go."

So, with a long sigh he went and called up Jerry, telling him he wouldn't be over to play ball.

On his way over to Mark's house he wondered to himself, *How did I ever get myself into this? I should have just said no. I should have explained to Mom that I had already promised the guys. I'd much rather be playing ball. The boys will have such a good time, and there I'll be, stuck inside playing games.*

When he reached Mark's house, at least he didn't show how awful he felt.

"Hi, Micky!" Mark called when he saw him. "Aw, man, am I glad to see you! Look at this leg of mine. Here's a pen. Would you be the first to sign my cast?"

So Micky signed his name. Mark was so obviously glad to see him that it somehow made Micky feel a little better. Mark showed him some of the new games he had gotten and it seemed only a little while until it was time for Micky to go home. He was surprised to find he had had a good time after all. He said good-bye to Mark and walked home.

A few days later Mark was back in school. Micky was busy playing ball after school and soon forgot his visit with Mark. After he got his cast off, Mark often came down to watch the boys, although it was a few weeks before he could play with them and then only once in a while because his leg was still weak. Mark was a quiet boy but the guys liked him and he soon had many friends.

It was just ten days until the biggest ball game of the season. Everyone was excited. Jerry was catcher. Micky played third base.

And then it happened. With only seven days to go, Micky woke up feeling hot and scratchy. His throat hurt and his eyes burned. His mother came in and put her hand on his forehead, then stuck a thermometer in his mouth.

"Goodness! You can't go to school today," she said. Then she looked Micky over a little more closely and noticed a red rash on his chest.

"I believe you have the measles!" she exclaimed.

Micky felt so terrible it was a relief to stay in bed. During the next few days he hardly cared what happened and he didn't mind missing school at all. He didn't want to see anyone and he didn't want to do anything.

Finally the doctor said he was no longer contagious but he still couldn't go back to school for a while. Micky was beginning to feel better and was very tired of staying in bed.

One day Jerry stopped by to see him after school. "Tomorrow's the big day, Mick," he said. "The guys have really been practicing. We're sure gonna miss you. I'm awful sorry you can't be there. Well, I gotta run and get to practice." Jerry hurried on, and before Micky could think of anything to say, he was gone.

All Micky could think about the next day was the ball game. The sun was shining and he wanted more than anything to be at the ball park, even if he couldn't play. If only he could go and watch. But the doctor had warned his mother not to let him get up too soon. So he was stuck in the house with nothing to do and no one to do it with. He tried to coax his mother into changing her mind but it was no use. Any other day Jerry or one of the other guys could have come over, but they would all be at the game.

He tried to read. But mostly he watched the clock. It was 2:30. Finally, 3:00. The school bell would be ringing. The boys would rush out of class on their way to the park. Micky couldn't remember when he had felt worse. He was grouchy and angry at everyone. He pulled a toy away from

Jonny and made him cry. Then he felt angry at his mother when she scolded him.

Even having Julie around to tease would have been a help, but she was spending the night over at Pam's house.

Sometime later as he was looking out the window thinking about the ball game and wishing he could be there, the doorbell rang. He heard voices as his mother answered the door, and a few minutes later, there was Mark standing in the doorway.

"Mark! Hi!" Micky said, grinning. "What are you doing here? Aren't you supposed to be at the ball game?"

"I'm just a substitute," Mark answered. "Anyway, I thought you might kinda like to have some company. I mean, since Jerry is catcher and all." He opened the bag he had brought and took out some of his games.

"Man, am I ever glad to see you!" Micky exclaimed. "I mean, it was pretty bad having to miss the game and all. Not only that, I've played with everything in the house, including Jonny's trucks, so I sure am glad you brought something different."

"Yeah, I know," Mark said. "I felt the same way when I had my broken leg. It was great of you to visit me then. I knew you were supposed to be playing ball, and I didn't really know any of the other guys very well. I never told you this before," Mark went on, coming over to sit on Micky's bed, "but Mom called up some of the other boys but none of them would come over. Only you. But come on, I'll beat you in chess!"

Missing the game didn't seem so important after all. Not when Micky had a friend like Mark to spend the time with. As they set up the chess pieces, Micky found himself smiling. Suddenly he felt good all over. It wasn't such a bad day after all!

9

STRAY DOG

Julie's Sunday school teacher had just finished telling the class about the apostle Peter's vision as he stood on the rooftop of his house waiting for dinner. He didn't understand the vision at the time and as he was questioning God, messengers arrived at the door asking him to go with them and visit their master, Cornelius, a Roman centurion. Then Peter understood his vision. It had been to prepare him and make him willing to visit this stranger of a different nationality. It was through Peter's visit that Cornelius and his entire household came to know Jesus Christ.

"Have any of you ever had a vision?" the teacher asked.

The eight girls sitting in a semicircle all shook their heads.

"I haven't either," Mrs. Carter admitted. "But have you ever stopped to wonder if God doesn't often guide us by the thoughts He puts into our minds? But it is up to us to listen and obey!

"I had a strange experience last week," she continued after a pause. "I usually go to the beauty shop about once a month, and a girl named Tina always cuts my hair for me. Last week I felt I just must go to the beauty shop even though I had just been there the week before.

" 'This is ridiculous,' I tried to tell myself. 'I just *got* my hair cut.'

" 'Then get it washed and set,' a voice seemed to say to me.

" 'But it's only Tuesday,' I argued. 'I'll wait until Thursday. Then it will be nice for the weekend.'

" 'Go now!' the voice said so clearly I finally thought, *It must be the Lord trying to get through to me.* So I went.

"I had no sooner walked through the door than Tina came up to me and said in surprise, 'Mrs. Carter! Oh, I'm so glad you've come! I've been wanting to talk to someone, and you are always so good about listening to my problems.' Then as she washed and set my hair, she told me in tears that her husband was sick in the hospital. The doctor had said he would have to have surgery. She was almost sick with worry. I had a wonderful chance to share with her some things about God's love and concern for both her and her family.

"Later in the week I went over to her house to stay with her children while she was in the hospital. When she came home, after they were in bed and asleep, we talked some more. It was that night that she accepted Jesus Christ as her Saviour.

"But what if I hadn't listened when the Lord told me to get my hair done?

"Sometimes," Mrs. Carter continued, "it isn't that dramatic. Sometimes the Lord makes us think of someone we know so we can pray for them. Maybe they are unhappy or in trouble and need our prayers. But we have to listen when God speaks to us in this way and do what He tells us to do, whether it is to go see someone or to pray for them."

Julie thought this was all very interesting, but she doubted if the Lord spent much time talking to twelve-year-old girls, except through their consciences in what they *shouldn't* do. It was all right for Mrs. Carter. She had been a Christian for years and years.

The week at school passed and, busy with exams and school activities, Julie soon forgot the Sunday school lesson.

On Friday night there was a storm. Julie was sound asleep when a crack of thunder made her sit up in bed with a start, her heart pounding. She was sure it had hit something close, it had been so loud. She ran into the hall and met her father who reassured her that everything was OK.

Back in bed, she couldn't sleep. The storm passed and the moon came out, but still she tossed and turned. Her mind wandered. Pam had called the night before and said she wouldn't be going to church with them Sunday. They were leaving early Saturday to visit an aunt and uncle. She and Pam always sat together in Sunday school. She would miss her.

She remembered what her teacher had said about praying for those we thought of in case they were in need. So she prayed for Pam and as she was praying, she thought of Lori Wendell on the other side of the world. "It's daytime in the Philippines now," she said to herself. "I wonder what Lori is doing. She's not in school because it's Saturday there. Maybe she's swimming."

She tried again to sleep but she had never felt more wide awake. And she kept thinking about Lori, remembering letters she had had from her. As she thought about her, instead of feeling glad, a strange sadness seemed to come over her. She felt troubled and didn't know why.

"When the Lord brings someone into your mind, listen!" she suddenly remembered Mrs. Carter saying.

"Lord, I don't know why I keep thinking about

Lori," Julie prayed. "But if she is homesick or in some sort of trouble, help her." She also prayed for the rest of the Wendell family and their work, and even as she prayed she drowsed off to sleep.

A couple of weeks later, as Julie walked in the door from school, her mother handed her a letter from Lori. She sat down at the kitchen table with a glass of juice and began to read aloud.

Dear Julie,

Wow! Have we ever had some excitement around here! Last Saturday after chores we hurried down to the spring to swim. We played tag and water polo and all kinds of games until lunchtime. We were walking home from swimming when a strange black dog came running down the path toward us. His eyes were red and wild-looking, and saliva dripped from his jaws. He ran past some little kids pulling a wagon but before he could reach us, Rusty, our German Shepherd, raced out from the house, barking like crazy. The dog tried to dart past him toward us, but Rusty kept barking and chasing him. The two dogs fought together until finally the black dog ran away.

We were so startled we just stood there watching, which was really dumb. We should have rushed into the house and locked the door. Anyway, our housemother came out to see what the commotion was about just as the dog ran away.

Rusty came up to her wagging his tail, but his face and shoulder were streaked with blood. She got a basin of water and soap and cleaned him up and we went and changed for lunch. We were just finishing when Mr. Graden, the superintendent in charge of the grounds and the workmen, came in.

"Any of you kids see that black dog that was running around?" he asked. And we told him what had happened. "He didn't get near any of you, did he?" he asked sharply, a frown on his face. So we told him that Rusty had kept him away from us. He was quiet for a few minutes then told us what had happened.

Someone had reported the dog to him, and he had grabbed a crowbar and jumped on his motorcycle to try to find the dog. Just then he saw the dog running toward his house, so he yelled to his wife to get their son. She ran to the porch, grabbed their three-year-old, and slammed the front door just as the dog ran up onto the porch.

Mr. Graden chased him on his cycle and saw him run into another house. He yelled to the girls staying there to stay out of the dog's way and the dog ran into their living room. Thinking he had him cornered, and hoping to shut the door on him, Mr. Graden walked slowly up to the house, crowbar in hand. Just as he reached the door, the dog sprang at him. Without even thinking, Mr. Graden swung the crowbar, hitting him in midair, stunning him. He hit him again before he could get up, and this time the blow killed the dog.

"We won't need a lab test of his brain to see he was definitely rabid," he said. "Luckily not a single person was bitten, although he ran past a number of people, including the little kids next door."

"What about Rusty?" our housefather asked quietly. "He fought with the dog to keep him away from the kids, and I'm afraid he was bitten on the shoulder and face."

We all held our breath, wondering what Mr. Graden would say. Rusty loves kids and is always ready to race or play ball with us. Surely he would be OK. He'd only been slightly wounded.

"When was his last rabies shot?" Mr. Graden asked.

Mrs. Winston went to check. When she came back and told him, Mr. Graden frowned and looked unhappy. But he didn't say anything, so we thought it was going to be OK.

We went on a long hike in the afternoon up a nearby mountain. It was fun but we were exhausted by the time we got home about dark.

The first thing I noticed when I reached the house was that Rusty didn't come bounding out to meet us. We called and called but he wasn't anywhere around. Then Mr. Winston told us all to come in and sit down.

"Kids," he said, "Rusty is dead. We took him over to a rancher's this afternoon. He shot him."

The kids groaned and the little ones started to cry. I had such a lump in my throat I couldn't swallow.

"The dog that bit him was definitely rabid, and it bit Rusty around the face. Even though Rusty had been vaccinated, we aren't sure if the vaccine itself was any good. We couldn't take a chance. If Rusty did develop rabies, he could spread it to you children before he himself developed the symptoms. We would have had to pen him up for a couple of weeks to make sure. And you know how he would have hated that!"

Everyone was crying now. Even Mr. Winston had tears in his eyes.

"We buried Rusty in the backyard," Mr. Winston continued. "And I thought maybe you boys might like to make and carve a small wooden headstone. The boys nodded.

Sunday afternoon they got to work and finished it after school on Monday.

It said, "RUSTY, a dog. He gave his life for his friends."

During devotions after supper that night, Mrs. Winston said, "In our sadness about Rusty, we have overlooked something. No one was bitten by that rabid dog! Anti-rabies vaccine is very hard to get, and we never know how effective it will be since it might be out of date. If that dog had bitten any of you, especially around the neck or face—" She paused and looked around the room. "You could have died from it!"

It was then I realized something I had forgotten in the excitement. I had been closest to the black dog. If Rusty hadn't run in front of me, that dog would have lunged right at me!

The Lord used Rusty to protect me!

Love ya!
Lori

"Oh, Mom, isn't that terrible!" Julie exclaimed when she had finished reading the letter to her mother. "That was only a couple of weeks ago. Let's see, her letter was written on March 18, a Monday, and this happened the Saturday before." She paused, thinking back.

"Hey, that would have been Friday night here. Wasn't that the night of the thunderstorm?" Her mother nodded. Julie was thoughtful, remembering. That was the night she couldn't sleep. She had kept thinking about Lori. In fact, it was only after she had prayed for her and the Wendells that she had fallen asleep.

She could hardly wait for Sunday. She wanted to share Lori's letter with Mrs. Carter and the girls and tell them Mrs. Carter had been right. Sometimes God did bring someone to your mind when they were in trouble. But it was important to listen!

10

THE PRETTIEST GIRL

Her name was Cynthia Louise and she was the prettiest girl in the seventh grade. In fact, Julie thought, she was just about the prettiest girl she had ever seen in her life. Her hair was long and the color of vanilla ice cream and she had the biggest, bluest eyes you could ever imagine.

"Call me Cindy Lou," she purred in a low voice to the kids that crowded around her on her first day of school, two weeks after everyone else had started. Boys and girls alike all wanted to be the first to show her around the school. Everyone wanted to make her feel welcome. Julie was the most thrilled of all because Cindy Lou was sitting next to her in class. Even boys from the upper grades flocked around Cindy Lou, eager to know her better.

Several days after her first day at school, Cindy

called Julie on the phone. "Honey," she said, "I'm having a terrible time with my math assignment. Think you could help me out?"

"I'll be glad to," Julie said and ran upstairs to get her book before leaving for Cindy's house. For the next half hour Julie patiently explained to Cindy Lou all about the math assignment. It was hard for Cindy to understand, but Julie decided that was probably because she had missed the first two weeks of school.

Many times in the weeks that followed, Cindy called Julie for help with her homework. It wasn't always math. Sometimes it was social studies, or lit. Cindy Lou had no trouble making friends, but she did have a time learning her lessons.

One day when Cindy called Julie, it wasn't to talk about homework. "Say, Julie, I'm giving a party next Friday night. Think you can come? It'll start at 7:30 here at my house. Do say you'll come!"

"Just a minute," Julie said, so excited she felt like jumping up and down. "I'll go ask Mom."

Mrs. Monroe was in the kitchen fixing supper. "Mom, Cindy is giving a party on Friday, can I go? Can I? Huh?"

"I suppose so. Who will be there?"

"All the kids," Julie answered, impatient to get back to the phone.

"But there will be some adults there, won't there?"

"I'm sure her mother will be there," Julie said hurriedly. " 'Course her father won't 'cause they're divorced."

"I guess you can go," Julie's mom said. But before she had finished speaking, Julie had raced back to the phone to tell Cindy she could come.

About an hour later, Julie had another call. This time from Pam.

"I haven't seen you much lately, Julie," she said. "When I look for you, you're always with Cindy. But would you come spend the night Friday? We can go swimming and take a picnic lunch to the park on Saturday."

"Oh, I'm sorry, Pam, I can't. Cindy just invited me to a party she is giving Friday."

"Oh." Pam didn't say anything for a minute and then in a small voice she said, "OK, then. See you in school." And before Julie could think of anything else to say, she had hung up.

Julie was so excited about the party she thought Friday would never come. It was a real honor to be invited to Cindy Lou's party. All the important kids from school would be there. She saw very little of Pam these days. Sometimes her conscience hurt a bit, but after all, there were other girls for Pam to play with. And Cindy *was* just about the nicest girl in school! Besides, by always hanging around Cindy, she was meeting all kinds of kids she had never met before, even kids from upper grades.

Friday night finally arrived. Julie had a new dress she had begged and pleaded her mother into buying for her. At 7:15, her father drove her over to Cindy's house.

"See you at ten," he said, as she got out. "Have a good time," she heard him call, as she ran up the steps.

Although she was a few minutes early, many other kids had gotten there before her. Cindy's mother was standing at the door.

"Come in," she smiled. Cindy's mother looked a lot like Cindy, but you could tell she was much older.

The other kids were sitting around drinking Cokes and playing games or just gabbing. Julie joined them, although she had never met many of the older boys before.

Sometime later, Cindy's mother came up to her and said, "You have a good time, now, but I'm going out for a while. You don't mind, do you?"

"No, that's OK," Cindy said, but Julie thought she sounded disappointed.

Cindy's mother got her coat and left.

"Cindy," Julie asked, "isn't your mother going to be here tonight?"

Cindy shrugged. "Oh, she has a date, I guess. She'll be back later on. Never mind. We'll have a good time, even without her."

Then Cindy got the fellows to push back the chairs and put on some loud rock music.

"Come on, let's dance!" she shouted to the kids above the din of the music. The dancing turned into a game where the boys would chase the girls and demand a kiss in payment when they caught them.

Julie was standing to one side watching. She wasn't sure she wanted to play. Just then Cindy came up to her.

"You don't look like you're having a good time, Julie. Isn't this just about the greatest party you've ever been at?" She took Julie by the hand to lead her out to the middle of the room.

"Come on out and let one of these fellows catch you. It's fun. You'll see."

"Guess I'd rather watch, Cindy," Julie said, pulling her hand away.

"Suit yourself, honey," Cindy shrugged. Then she giggled as one of the boys suddenly caught her and kissed her.

Just then there was a commotion at the door as Mac and two of his pals pushed into the room.

"Hi, Cindy!" Mac called. "We brought some fun to liven up your party. Bring it in, boys." He nudged his companions who stepped outside and returned with a case of beer.

Looking at Mac made Julie wish she were home. She pushed back against the wall, hoping the boys wouldn't notice her. Cindy was smiling up at Mac, although her face looked flushed.

"Julie."

Hearing her name, Julie turned toward the door. Her father was standing there waiting to take her home. She couldn't remember when she had been so glad to see anyone!

"My goodness!" Cindy exclaimed, turning from Mr. Monroe in the doorway to Julie. "You aren't going to leave already, are you? The party's hardly gotten started." She giggled as she looked toward Mac, who grinned in agreement.

"I'm sorry, Cindy, but I have to go now," Julie said, getting her coat.

"OK, see you next week."

"Uh, Cindy, you said you wanted help with your homework tomorrow. Shall I come over?" Julie asked.

"Yeah, OK. But don't come over until afternoon, you hear? I'll be sleeping all morning." And Cindy said good night.

When Julie got home, her mother was waiting

for her. "Hi!" she said, taking her coat. "Have a good time?"

"I guess so," Julie answered.

"What's wrong? You don't sound too sure."

"It was a great party. We had a great time," Julie said, forcing a laugh. "I'm kinda tired. Guess I'll get right to bed."

"Good night, Julie," her mother said, giving her a quick hug and kissing her cheek.

The next afternoon, Julie hurried over to Cindy's house, her arms full of books.

Cindy was in the bedroom. "Come on up, Julie," she called. "We don't have to do that old homework right now. Sit down and let's just visit a while."

Cindy was brushing her hair.

"Oh, Cindy, I think you have the prettiest hair I ever saw. It's such a beautiful color."

Cindy Lou laughed. "This? Oh, Honey! You're the cutest. You know this isn't my real hair. I mean, it's my real hair but the color's not real. Why if I left it its natural color, it would be the dullest brown you ever saw. Nope, my blonde hair comes out of a bottle." And she laughed again.

"You mean it's not naturally blonde?" Julie sounded surprised.

"Of course not. But who cares? It's much prettier this way, don't you think?"

Just then Cindy reached into her dressing table and took out a package of cigarettes. "Here, Julie, have a cigarette."

"Uh, I don't smoke, Cindy," Julie said, feeling her face getting hot.

"You don't? Why ever not?" Cindy asked in a surprised voice, her eyebrows raised.

"Well, uh, no one in our family smokes; and, well, my folks always said it wasn't good for me," Julie answered, twisting a corner of her skirt.

"Not good for you? Why ever not?" Cindy was incredulous.

"It can hurt my health."

"Hurt your health? One little cigarette? Oh, come on. Now look at my mother. She's been smoking two packs a day for years, and she's still going strong. One little cigarette isn't going to hurt anything."

"I don't know. It just doesn't seem right somehow."

"Now you listen here," Cindy said, coming over to stand beside Julie's chair. "I know you go to church and are very religious, but did your mother ever show you one single place in your Bible where it said, 'Thou shalt not smoke one cigarette'?"

"Well, no—"

"If your Bible doesn't say there's anything wrong with it, why do you? Your mother just doesn't

93

know. If she doesn't smoke, she doesn't have any idea what it's like. Now, come on. Try it for yourself. You can decide. If you don't like it, that's up to you. Here, I'll light it for you."

Cindy lit a cigarette and gave it to Julie.

"Here. Let me show you. You just hold it this way and take little puffs. Don't take too deep a breath, you might choke."

Julie tried it. It wasn't so great after all. In fact, it burned her throat.

"See?" Cindy said, lighting one for herself. "I knew once you tried it, you'd like it."

"It's OK, I guess." She put the cigarette in Cindy's gold ashtray and gathered up her books. "I'd better go now," she said hurriedly.

"See you in class," Cindy said.

It wasn't until she was halfway home that Julie remembered they hadn't done any homework. Oh, well. She remembered other times she had been at Cindy's house helping her with homework. Sometimes it seemed like she did most of Cindy's work for her. In fact, she did almost everything except write the answers on Cindy's paper. Cindy didn't seem to be interested in her studies.

"In fact," Cindy had told her one day, "I'm supposed to be in eighth grade, but I had this old meany of a teacher who didn't pass me. It's because of her that I'm behind."

Julie began to wonder about Cindy. She still thought she was the prettiest girl she had ever seen, but she wasn't sure if she was the best friend she ever had or not.

She felt awful about the cigarette she had smoked. It was true she didn't know any verse in the Bible that said it was wrong to smoke, but her parents had always taught her it was bad for her health. They had said that, since her body belonged to Jesus Christ, she should take extra good care of it. Just thinking about it made her feel kind of sick inside.

When she got home, her mother met her at the door.

"Hi, sweetie! Have a good time?" Then she saw the downcast look on Julie's face. "What's the matter? Not sick, are you?"

"Just tired, I guess," Julie answered, not looking at her mother. "I'll go up to my room until supper."

At supper she hardly ate a thing. "What's the matter, Julie?" her mother asked. "Fried chicken and apple pie have always been favorites of yours."

"Hey, can I have your pie?" Micky asked. "Can I? Huh?"

"I guess so," Julie answered, passing it to him.

"You *must* be sick," her mother said, getting up to feel her forehead. "I've never known you to pass up apple pie before." You go lie down and I'll be up soon."

Julie went upstairs. She felt sick, all right. She felt sick about the night before, about all the things the kids had been doing. She felt sick about Pamela who had wanted her to spend the night at her house. She felt sick about the cigarette she had tried, when she knew she shouldn't. She put her head in her pillow and burst into tears.

Her mother found her sobbing when she came up a few minutes later.

"Oh, Julie, what *is* the matter?" she asked, sitting beside her and smoothing her hair. "Like to tell me about it?"

"Oh, Mom! You know that, ever since I met Cindy, it seems like things haven't been going right. I wanted to be a friend to her. She was so nice and so popular and so pretty. I wanted to help her with her homework so she could get better grades and pass. I was so excited about the party last night. But it wasn't much fun at all. Their games were rowdy, and there were kids there I had never seen before. They were running after the girls and kissing them. Then, just before I left, Mac and two of his friends came with a case of beer."

"Where was Cindy's mother while all of this was going on?" Julie's mother asked quietly.

"I thought she would be there, and she was when

I arrived. But she left a little later on a date and never came back."

"You mean she wasn't there the whole evening?"

"No. And the kids got kinda rough. I was glad when Dad came to get me, even though Cindy said I was silly to go home so early."

"Cindy isn't as fortunate as you are," Julie's mother said quietly. "Since her parents are divorced, she probably sees very little of her father. And her mother is so busy having a good time that she probably doesn't pay much attention to Cindy. Maybe that's why Cindy doesn't care about her schoolwork but just tries to have a good time like her mother."

"Oh, Mom! All this time I've hardly talked to Pam. She called and wanted me to spend the night last night, and I wouldn't." Julie's shoulders shook. "I made her sad and I'm sorry."

"Sweetie, you can call her up and tell her you're sorry. She'll understand."

Julie started to cry even harder, so that for a few minutes she couldn't talk. Her mother just sat quietly beside her, stroking her hair.

"Mom, that's not the worst of it," she said at last when she could talk again. "When I was at Cindy's house this afternoon, I smoked a cigarette. She told me it would be great and I should try it. She told me that, if I didn't smoke I wouldn't know what it was like. She said the Bible didn't say it was wrong, so why did I say it was. So I smoked it. And I'm sorry. I feel terrible."

"Honey, I'm so relieved that you've felt free to tell me these things. You see, one cigarette probably won't hurt you. It might only make you feel a little funny or sick. But one cigarette often leads to two which leads to three and so on. By the time you are smoking many a day, you find you can't stop, at least not very easily. And smoking many cigarettes over a period of months and years *can* hurt your health."

"Mom, Cindy said her mom has been smoking two packs a day for a long time, and it hasn't hurt her!"

"But how do you know it hasn't hurt her? How do you know how well she really is? And how do you know she might not die much sooner than she otherwise would?"

"Anyway, Mom, I'm sorry. I knew you didn't like it, and that was the worst part of all."

"Honey, I forgive you. Would you like to pray and ask Jesus to forgive you too?"

So Julie prayed. Then she said, "You know, Mom, Cindy is kinda like that big, red apple I had in my lunch yesterday. It looked big and juicy and delicious, but when I bit into it, I found out it was rotten."

"Do you suppose that's because she doesn't know Jesus as her Saviour? Maybe she would go to church with you sometime."

"Maybe," Julie agreed. "But now I gotta call Pam."

The happiness in Pam's voice as she talked to her made Julie feel happy too. They agreed to walk to church together the next morning, and Julie invited Pam home with her for dinner.

Julie was humming a favorite song as she hung up the phone and went skipping upstairs to tell her mother about her plans. She didn't feel one bit sick. In fact, she felt hungry.

"Any pie left, Mom?" she asked.

Her mother laughed. "Come on, let's go see!"

11

BEAUTY IN A BOTTLE

"Cindy Lou really is a beautiful girl," Julie said to Pam one Friday afternoon about three weeks after Cindy's party. "She has more boyfriends than anyone else."

Pam agreed. "We have lots of friends, but we don't have boyfriends who take us to parties and things like Cindy's friends do."

The girls were sitting in Pam's room. Julie got up and went over to Pam's dresser, leaning forward to look at herself closely in the mirror.

"Maybe it's because she is so much prettier than we are," she said at last. "Maybe if we got to work on ourselves, we could make ourselves prettier and more popular."

Pam got off the bed and came over to stand behind Julie. "Let's see. Maybe we could think of a different hair style." And she started to brush and comb Julie's light brown hair.

For the next hour, the girls combed their hair every different way they could think of: parted in the middle, on the side, pulled back with barrettes, with a side flip, but nothing seemed to look just right.

"Maybe it's because our hair is just too ordinary," Julie said at last. "Everybody's hair looks like ours, just plain brown!" Cindy has beautiful hair, and the color is straight from a bottle! Why don't we color our hair?"

"I don't know." Pam wasn't nearly as excited about it as Julie. "It doesn't seem quite right, somehow."

"Did your mother ever tell you you couldn't dye your hair?"

"No, but—"

"My mother colors her hair to cover up all the gray. She says she feels young so why should she look old?"

Pam laughed. "My mom does the same. But maybe it's different with kids."

"When I get home tonight," Julie said, collecting her books, "I'll ask Mother if it's all right. If it is, I'll come over tomorrow and we can go to the drugstore together, buy some hair color, and make ourselves beautiful, OK?"

So the girls agreed.

As soon as Julie got home, she hurried to her

room, counted the money in her purse, decided it was enough, and hurried to find her mother.

"Mom," she said when she found her in the sewing room, "I know some things are a sin. You know, like cheating and lying. But how about other things, like some of the things Cindy does?"

Her mother was mending a rip in Micky's pants that he had gotten sliding out of a tree.

"What things?" she asked.

"You know what beautiful hair she has. She says it isn't her natural color; she gets it out of a bottle. I mean, is it wrong to put a rinse on your hair to make it brighter and prettier?"

"Not exactly. It's not a sin. God wants us to look our best. But I think He wants us to avoid extremes. The Bible talks about moderation in all things, and I think the girl who wears the shortest skirt and the heaviest makeup or the boy with the longest, messiest hair is not being moderate but extreme. Neither one really looks his best. There are many things we can do that aren't sins but just aren't very smart. Like those two pieces of cake Micky ate for supper last night. It didn't seem like such a good idea when he had a stomachache afterward! Coloring your hair isn't a sin, but it may just not be very smart. Why do you ask?"

"Oh, I just wondered," Julie said casually. "Guess I'll get on with my homework. Anything to eat?"

"Some chocolate cookies, but don't eat too many!" Her mother smiled. And Julie, remembering Micky, laughed.

Julie could hardly wait to get over to Pam's house the next day.

"It's OK. Mom says it's OK," she said as soon as she saw Pam.

"You mean your mother said it's OK for you to change the color of your hair?" Pam asked in surprise.

"Well, not exactly."

"OK," Pam said, "exactly what *did* your mother say?"

"She said it wasn't a sin to color your hair."

"But did she say *you* could color *your* hair?"

"No. I was afraid to ask her."

"Oh, Julie!" Pam sounded disgusted. "If you didn't ask her—"

Julie interrupted. "I thought we could go ahead and color my hair. When I get home and Mother sees how beautiful it looks, she'll be glad we did it. Besides, by then it will be done and she won't be able to do anything about it. Anyway, she did say it wasn't a sin; and besides, it's *my* hair!"

"I don't know." Pam didn't sound convinced.

"Mom said God wants us to look our best, and that's all I'm trying to do. Come on, don't be chicken."

"OK, but don't you think we should get some advice on color and stuff?"

"No, we'll go to the drugstore, pick the color we like best, and just buy it! You know that all the ads say how easy it is. You just rub it in, wait a while, rinse it out, and it's in for good—well, for a month or so anyway."

At the drugstore, the girls found there were indeed a lot of colors to choose from.

"We don't want blonde like Cindy Lou, and we don't want black. They're too extreme," Julie said, looking at the chart.

"But that still leaves an awful lot in between," Pam observed. "Here's a pretty red. Like to be a redhead?"

"That's too bright. Maybe we should get a color closer to my own. It's already light brown, but I want it to be special."

"Here's one that's really beautiful," Pam said. "It's called 'glowing auburn.'"

"Oh, yes! I like that one," Julie agreed and quickly bought it before Pam could make her change her mind.

Back at Pam's house, the girls carefully read the directions and did just what it said. They borrowed Pam's mother's rubber gloves, rubbed the color in Julie's hair, waited, shampooed and set it, then dried it.

At last it was time to comb it out. Pam made Julie sit still while she took out the rollers.

"Oh, Julie!" she said at last when the last curler was out. "It's—well, it's bright all right."

Julie didn't say a word. She just sat in stunned silence and stared at herself.

"Oh, dear!" she said at last in a small voice. "It's so *orange!* That's not the color on the box. Why does it look like this? It's awful! Who ever heard of anyone with bright orange hair?"

"You'll be the only one in school with hair that color," Pam said, trying to be helpful.

"I just thought it would be the most beautiful reddish brown. But this!" Then she had another thought. "What am I going to tell Mom?" And she put her head down on her arms.

"I don't know, Julie, but you'd better think of something soon," Pam said.

"I'd better get home and get it over with," Julie moaned.

"Guess I'd better get busy with my homework," Pam said.

"Oh no you don't, Pamela! You come with me! You helped me, and now you've got to help me explain to my mother."

"It was *your* idea, Julie. If you remember, *I* was the one who didn't think it was so great!"

"Yeah, I know. You're right. But please come with me, Pam," she begged.

"Oh, all right."

As the girls were going out the door, Julie suddenly realized that everyone they passed on the sidewalk would see her hair.

"Oh, Pam! I can't go like this. Loan me a scarf, will you?"

Pam brought a scarf and put it on Julie.

"Pull it down over my forehead and tuck it in the sides."

"But you look so funny!"

On the way out the door they met Pam's father who looked curiously at Julie but didn't say anything.

They found Julie's mother in the kitchen. "Hi, girls! Come on in," she greeted them, looking up from the cake she was icing. "Julie, why on earth do you have your scarf on like that?"

"Oh, Mom!" Julie wailed. "This is why," and she pulled off the scarf, exposing her bright new hair.

"Good grief, Julie! Whatever did you do to your hair?" her mother said, aghast.

"You said God wanted us to look our best, and it wasn't wrong to color your hair. And my hair seemed so drab I wanted to change it to a pretty color. So I got money I was saving and bought a rinse, and Pam helped me put it on. But it didn't turn a pretty golden color, it turned this horrible orange."

"Honey, why didn't you ask me first?" her mother moaned.

"I was afraid you'd say no because we're too young to color our hair."

"You're right," her mother agreed. "That's exactly what I would have said."

"I wanted to surprise you, Mom, I really did," Julie said, starting to cry. "I wanted to come home and have my hair look so nice," she sobbed. "I wanted to surprise the kids at school, too. I wanted to look my best so the boys would like me—"

"Good grief, Julie!" Micky whooped just then as he came into the kitchen. "Whatever happened to your hair? Is it ever a mess!" He was bent double with laughter.

"Now Micky, that's enough!" his mother said. "There'll be no more comments out of you."

"But, Mom, her hair! That's the brightest orange I've ever seen! Oh, Julie!" He could hardly talk he was laughing so hard. "Wait till the fellows see you!"

"Mom, make him stop! Make him stop!" Julie begged. "Go away!" she hollered, trying to push Micky out the door.

"Michael! Get yourself something to eat and leave Julie alone," their mother said. "Julie, come on upstairs," she said to her, taking her by the hand.

"We've a carrot top in the family. Carrots! Carrots!" Micky chanted.

"Michael! I won't tell you again!" his mother said as she pulled Julie out the door. Pam followed closely behind.

Upstairs in Julie's bedroom, her mother shut the door and sat down.

"Now what can we do about your hair? Let's try washing it."

"It's no use, Mrs. Monroe," Pam said. "The label said it was permanent—at least for several weeks."

Julie's mother shook her head. "Julie, I did say this wasn't a sin. But do you remember what else I said? I said some things just weren't very smart. This is one of them."

"I know, Mom, and I'm sorry. But it looks terrible! What'll I do?"

"If it won't wash out, I guess you'll just have to go to school like this."

"I won't! The kids would all laugh. I won't **go** at all. I'll just lock myself in my room!" Julie threw herself on the bed and started sobbing again.

"There, honey, we'll think of something," her mother said, putting her arm around her shoulders.

"I know," she said at last, snapping her fingers.

"Viv! I'll call Viv at the beauty shop. Maybe she can put on another rinse to tone it down."

She left the room and was back in a couple of minutes. We're in luck. Even though it's Saturday afternoon, Viv thinks she can squeeze you in. But we've got to go right now. Come on, Pam. I'll drop you off at home on the way," Mrs. Monroe said, hurrying out the door.

And so Julie went through the whole bit again: the hair color, the long wait, the shampoo, and the set. But when it was finished, it did look much better. Not quite natural, but a definite improvement. Through all the long afternoon, Julie kept thinking about her pretty brown hair. It hadn't been so bad after all. Not exotic like blonde or orange, but really quite nice.

"Thanks so much, Viv," Mrs. Monroe said, when she had paid her and they were going out the door.

"Anytime you want your hair color changed," Viv said to Julie, "you check with me and your mother first."

"That'll be a long, long time," Julie answered. Her mother and Viv just smiled.

12

THE BULLY

Micky and Julie felt sad and excited at the same time. Even though it was the middle of the school year, their dad had been transferred to another city, Weston, and they had moved. This was their first day at their new school.

Micky was excited as he started out, wondering what new friends he would make that day. But when he returned that afternoon, his once clean shirt was dirty and torn. He walked by himself, his hands in his pockets, kicking the sidewalk. The day had been a disaster. He had met Butch.

During recess that day, Butch had come up to Micky and taunted, "Ha! Look at the new kid! You sure don't look like much!"

He had hit him across the shoulders so hard that Micky almost fell down. Then he had laughed and laughed.

"What's your name, kid?" he asked.

"My friends call me Micky," Micky told him.

"Ha! I'm going to call you Shrimp." He gave Micky a shove that sent him sprawling. Then, laughing loudly, he and the other boys had gone off.

That was the beginning of an almost daily nightmare for Micky. Julie had made many friends and spent most of her time with them, so Micky had to walk to and from school by himself. On the way, he had to pass Butch's house. If Butch was home, he always managed to see Micky coming, no matter how quiet Micky tried to be.

One time he hid behind the hedge in front and when Micky came by, he stuck out a long stick. Micky fell and cut his lip. Another time, he threw some soft rotten tomatoes at him that spattered all over his shirt. Every time he could, Micky went around the block to avoid Butch's house; but, sometimes when he was running late, there was nothing else to do but pass the house. And if he was late, Butch always seemed to be later.

Things were no better at school. During recess, Butch and his friends either mocked and teased him or ignored him. If one of the other guys tried to be friendly with Micky, Butch would get so angry the boy never tried again.

One day, Butch put ants in Micky's lunch so he couldn't eat it. Another time he hid his math book in the bushes so Micky had to spend all of recess looking for it.

Micky couldn't remember when he had been so miserable. More than anything in the world he wanted to be back at his old school. He missed Jerry and his friends.

He called Jerry on the phone one Sunday afternoon to catch up on all the news.

"They arrested Mac and his Pack for giving drugs to kids at the junior high," Jerry told him. "They caught him at it so he doesn't have a chance. Dad says he'll go to jail for sure. That's the last we've seen of *him*," Jerry added, a note of satisfaction in his voice. Neither of the boys knew then how wrong he was or what a big part they would play in Mac's life.

But the phone call only made Micky more homesick. He felt so awful that he didn't care about anything. When he was in class, he couldn't think about anything except how much he missed Jerry and how much he dreaded walking home afterward. His grades were terrible, and his teacher wrote his parents a note about them.

That night his dad came in and sat down on his bed to talk to him. He had hardly mentioned his grades when Micky, much to his dismay, began to cry. He cried so hard he couldn't talk. His father just sat there with his arm around him until he could calm down a little. Finally he managed to sob out the whole story. He told about the time Butch had spilled ink all over his homework and he had had to stay after school and do it over. And about the time Butch told the teacher that Micky had emptied the wastebasket on her desk, when he had done it himself. The teacher had made him stay after school three days and wash the blackboards as punishment.

"Dad, no matter what I do or how hard I try, he still teases me. I want to go back to Springdale!" And he began to cry harder.

"Maybe I could go and talk to the teacher."

"That wouldn't do any good," Micky said between sobs. "It would just make Butch angry, and then I'd really be in for it."

"Micky, I don't know what to do except pray about it. Maybe the Lord will give you a chance to show kindness to Butch. It sounds like he needs a big dose of it."

"Show kindness to Butch? It wouldn't do any good! It would be like trying to clean up a mud puddle by pouring in soap. The soap would sink to the bottom and the puddle would be just as dirty as ever!"

"Maybe so, but it can't hurt to give it a try."

"I guess you're right. Things can't get much worse!"

But he was wrong. The next day, Miss Engle-stein was missing some money from her desk, and Butch said he had seen Micky take it. Angry, the teacher had searched Micky's desk. Then she had made him come up in front of the class and turn out his pockets to prove he didn't have the money. He was sent to the principal; but because there was no proof that he had taken the money, he was sent back to his class.

That night Micky told his father all that had happened. He also told him that he absolutely was *not* going back to school.

His father had to talk a long time, but at last he persuaded him to give it another try.

"You have something very wonderful that not all the Butches in the world can take away from you," he told Micky. "And that is Jesus Christ as your Friend and Saviour. You don't think Butch is a Christian, do you?"

"Butch?! Not him. He wouldn't darken the door of a church if you paid him!"

"We know Jesus loves you and He also loves Butch. Maybe the Lord will use you to change his mind."

Micky wasn't convinced, but he did feel a little better after praying about it.

The next day Butch was sick; and, although he wouldn't admit it to anyone, Micky had never been

114

so glad about anything. It gave him a breathing spell.

That day Miss Englestein announced that the midterm spelling test would be given that Friday, and she warned everyone to study.

During recess the next day, Micky was being careful to stay out of sight because Butch was back in school. Butch and some of his friends were sitting under a tree; and Micky heard Butch say, "Yeah, guess that's one book I'll have to open before Friday. My old man told me if I flunk this spelling test, he's going to take his belt and lick the daylights out of me." He sighed. "He'll do it too!"

Butch was so wrapped up in his own problems that for the next few days he simply ignored Micky.

On Thursday afternoon, Micky had to go to the school library to work on a book report. It was an interesting book; and when Micky finally looked up to check the clock, he saw that it was almost the four-o'clock closing time.

Micky finished his work and put everything away. Then he picked up his books, including his spelling book, and went to the coatrack to get his jacket. There something caught his eye. He went over to look closer. It was a spelling book that had fallen between the rack and the wall. Inside in big letters he saw the name BUTCH MASTERS. The spelling test was the next day. If Butch flunked it, he'd really get it from his father.

It would serve him right. It was time someone gave Butch a whipping. All the mean things Butch had done to him the last few weeks passed through his mind. He would just put the book back where he had found it, go out, and close the door. He glanced at the clock. In ten minutes the janitor would lock up the school; and then, even if Butch did notice he had forgotten his book, it would be too late to do anything about it. Butch would just be out of luck.

Micky started to put the book back in the crack between the rack and the wall. But, somehow inside, he knew it wasn't the right thing to do. He wanted to, but yet he knew he shouldn't. He knew he should stop at Butch's house on his way home and give him the book. He stood there holding the book. It seemed like there were two voices inside him.

One was saying, "Leave it, leave it! It's not up to you to see that Butch remembers his spelling book. If he's careless, that's his fault."

The other voice seemed to say, "Just because Butch is a bully, it doesn't mean you should do something you know is wrong. And besides, haven't you been praying for Butch? Maybe this is the chance you've been waiting for."

But the first voice answered, "Even if you did give him his spelling book, it wouldn't do any good. He'd still be mean to you."

"How do you know unless you try?" the second voice seemed to answer.

It was getting late. He had to be out by 4 o'clock. Grabbing the book and his things, Micky hurried out the door, pulling it shut behind him before he could change his mind and return Butch's book to the rack.

He hurried down the steps, trying not to think about how scared he was and trying not to notice how hard his heart was pounding. The last thing in the world he wanted to do at that moment was to stop at Butch's house. He wanted to run home as fast as he could. Maybe Butch's mother would come to the door, and he could just give it to her and run.

No such luck. He had no sooner rung the door-bell than Butch himself opened it. Micky was shaking so hard that he could hardly talk. So, instead, he held out the spelling book and stammered, "I— I found it. Down by the coatrack. Thought you might need it."

"My spelling book! So that's where it was. I've been looking all over for it. I was sure I had it in the pile of books I brought home."

"I gotta run," Micky said, turning to go down the steps.

"Wait!" Butch ordered.

Micky turned back, wondering what was coming next, ready to duck in case Butch decided to let him have it.

There was a strange look on Butch's face. "But why did you bring this to me?" he asked.

"I heard you tell the fellows that, if you flunked the test, you'd get a whipping from your dad; so I figured you'd need it."

"But after all I've done to you, why didn't you just leave it there? Didn't you want to get even with me?" he asked.

"Yes. Yes, I did!" Micky admitted. "While I was thinking about what to do, I remembered just about everything you've done to me since that first day of school; and I just about put the book back. I thought it would serve you right if your dad *did* lick you. But then I remembered something my best Friend said about loving your enemies, and I knew He would want me to bring it to you. So I picked it up and ran out fast before I could change my mind."

"Best friend?" Butch asked. "But you don't have any friends at school. I wouldn't let any of the fellows play with you. What friend is this?"

118

"Jesus is my Friend. My Saviour, too," Micky told him.

"You mean the Jesus we sing carols about at Christmas? But He's been dead thousands of years!"

"He did die on the cross, but He didn't stay dead. He's alive again and He's my best Friend."

"I wish I had a best Friend like that," Butch said wistfully. "But I've done so many bad things He'd never want to meet me."

"Sure He would. He loves you just as much as He does me, Butch."

"You're kidding!"

"No, honest. If you want to know more about Him, come to church with me next Sunday."

"Maybe I will." Butch stopped and was quiet for a minute. "Say, thanks for the book," he said at last.

"It's OK," Micky said. "I gotta run. Good luck with the spelling." And he ran down the steps and skipped all the way home. Maybe life in Weston wasn't going to be so bad after all!

13

MAC

The sign at the old McKeever place said: No Trespassing! But it was old and weather-beaten and had fallen off the tree into the underbrush below. Because bulldozers would soon come to clear the land for the new expressway, no one had bothered to replace the sign.

Jerry and Micky peered cautiously through the rotting fence. It was the first day of spring vacation and Micky had come from Weston to spend it with Jerry.

"Come on, Micky, let's go in. There's no one around."

But Micky wasn't so sure. "I don't know, Jerry, maybe we shouldn't. Junkies and pushers used to hang around here. Maybe some are still here!"

The boys were quiet, listening. But they heard only a few birds and the distant noise of traffic.

"Aw, it's deserted, Micky. Ever since the police raided the place ages ago, things have been quiet."

"OK, let's go," Micky suddenly agreed and led the way to a section of the fence that was rotten and broken down.

The boys pushed their way though the brush until they reached an overgrown path where the going was easier. As they neared the house, they saw evidence that someone had been there. Rusty beer cans and trash littered the yard. The house itself had a defeated, brooding air and smelled of decay and rotting wood. Someone had removed the door and shutters on the windows and the ground was charred from a long-ago fire.

"OK, we've seen it, let's go!" Micky breathed in a whisper.

Throwing his shoulders back and taking a deep breath, Jerry said in a voice that sounded loud in the stillness, "Come on, let's go inside."

Just then a sound made the boys stop suddenly, their hearts beating faster, the tiny hairs on their arms feeling prickly.

"What was that?" Micky asked, grabbing Jerry's arm.

It came again, a hoarse, agonized, "Help! O God! Somebody help me!"

"Someone's in there and needs help!" Jerry exclaimed.

"Let's get out of here!" And Micky started back toward the fence.

121

"Help me!" they heard again.

"Whoever it is, we can't just leave him," Jerry said.

Micky stopped and stood looking at the house, uncertain what to do. "Maybe it's a trick," he whispered.

"Help!"

"That doesn't sound like a trick," Jerry whispered back. "Maybe someone's hurt. We'd better go see."

"OK," Micky agreed and started cautiously back to the house.

Once inside, they looked around but saw no one. Then they heard a moan.

"We're coming!" Jerry called. "Where are you?"

"Here." The voice came from their right, through the hall. The floor was rotten and broken in places so the boys had to watch where they stepped. More trash and old pieces of broken furniture blocked the way.

"Hurry!" the voice called. Through the room at last, they came to another hall. There on the stairs, a figure was crouched, his arms across his stomach, moaning and rocking from side to side.

"What's the matter? Are you sick?" Micky asked, going closer. The young man lifted his head and Micky stared. Mac! His eyes were bloodshot and a stubby beard covered his face. He looked pale, and sweat ran down his cheeks, even though it was a cool day.

"Help me," he muttered hoarsely, clutching again at his stomach as another spasm shook him.

The boys got on either side of him to help him get up. "We'll get you out of here," they assured him. "Here, stand up."

"I can't," he groaned, pointing. It was then the boys noticed that the step had been broken and his right foot had caught between two jagged pieces of wood.

"We've got to move that piece of wood and free his foot," Micky exclaimed. But when they tried, Mac screamed in pain and they saw how red and swollen his bare ankle was above his tennis shoe.

"We've got to go for help," Jerry decided. "We'll go to the nearest house and call the police."

At that Mac lifted his head. "Not the fuzz!" he growled. The boys stepped back, alarmed at the fierce look on his face. But even as they watched, it faded, his eyes closed and he grimaced in pain. "A fix. My life for a fix—" he kept begging.

"I'll get Dad," Jerry decided. "He'll know what to do."

"I'll come with you," Micky agreed.

"No!" Mac shouted. "Don't leave me alone!" he pleaded, tears streaming down his cheeks.

Micky had never seen a man cry, and it made him feel strange inside.

"OK, I'll stay with you," he said. "Hurry, Jerry!" he called to his friend, who was already out the door.

There was nothing Micky could do, so he just sat down on the bottom step and looked at Mac.

With his eyes closed, Mac started mumbling, "A fix, came here for a fix—had one hidden upstairs—"

"Where are your friends, Mac?" Micky asked quietly.

"Friends!" Mac exclaimed, spitting at the rail in hate and disgust. "Some friends! They split when the cops busted me. Haven't seen them since. The fix— Those dirty skunks must've taken it. O God! How did I get like this?" Mac groaned again and to Micky's surprise began to sob, his face in his hands, his shoulders shaking.

"It isn't God's fault you're here," Micky said.

"Huh? What'd you say, kid?" Mac lifted a haggard face to look at Micky.

"I said, don't blame God. It isn't His fault you're here." He paused a moment, thinking. Then he added, "But my dad says it doesn't matter who you are or what you've done, God still loves you."

"What does your dad know about me and God?" Mac asked, looking curiously at Micky.

"A lot. We've been praying for you, for ages and

ages. In fact, Julie and I kinda gave up, thinking it was hopeless; but Dad said no one is ever hopeless with God."

"You're kidding!" Mac stared in disbelief. "You praying for me!" His laughter sounded wild and desperate, and Micky was suddenly scared. Then the laugh broke into a sob. "It's too late, kid. Even God can't help me now!"

Micky remembered all the times he had seen Mac proud and swaggering. He remembered what a bully he was. This figure huddled on the steps didn't seem like the same person.

"How do you know He can't help you unless you ask Him?" Micky asked at last, putting his hand timidly on Mac's shoulder.

Just then the sound of voices came from the front and Jerry hurried in with his dad.

"An ambulance is coming," Mr. Schaff assured them, as he bent over to look at Mac's leg. He had brought some tools with him, and as carefully as possible he freed Mac's ankle.

"I'll go with him to the hospital," Mr. Schaff said quietly when the ambulance arrived. "See you boys later."

The boys went back to Jerry's house and tried to shoot baskets, but they kept thinking about Mac, wondering what was happening to him.

They had just sat down to lunch when Jerry's

dad called to say Mac was in surgery. Doctors were setting his ankle, which was broken. "I think I'll stay until he's awake," Mr. Schaff added. "It's hard not to have any relatives or friends who care."

The boys stayed close to the house, hoping Jerry's dad would call again, but instead, about mid-afternoon, he drove up to the house.

"How is he?" both boys asked at once.

"He's going to be OK," Mr. Schaff assured them, putting an arm around each of their shoulders and heading for the house. "But the strangest thing happened," he added, looking curiously at the boys. As he was waking up, Mac kept saying over and over, 'He'll help me. He'll help me. I know He will. I asked Him to!' "

The boys looked at each other as they walked into the house. They had so much to tell Mr. Schaff! Micky could hardly wait to tell Julie that God *had* answered their prayers!